THE SPARTAN TRIGGER
BRYCE ALLEN

BEDLAM PRESS
2014

FIRST TRADE PAPERBACK EDITION

THE SPARTAK TRIGGER
© 2014 by Bryce Allen
Cover art © 2014 by Erik Wilson

This edition © 2014 Bedlam Press

ISBN: 978-1-939065-59-9

Assistant Editors:
Amanda Baird

Book design & typesetting:
David G. Barnett
Fat Cat Graphic Design
www.fatcatgraphicdesign.com

Bedlam Press
an imprint of
Necro Publications
5139 Maxon Terrace
Sanford, FL 32771
www.necropublications.com

All rights reserved. No part of this publication may be reproduced, stored in a retrieval system, or transmitted in any form or by any means, digital, electronic, mechanical, photocopying, recordings or otherwise, or conveyed by the Internet or a website without prior written permission of the publisher or copyright holder, except in the case of brief quotations embodied in critical articles and reviews.

Names, characters, places, and incidents are the product of the author's imagination or are used fictionally. Any resemblance to actual events, locales, or persons, living or dead, is entirely coincidental.

10 9 8 7 6 5 4 3 2 1

THE SPARTAK TRIGGER

"What do you call your act?"

The drunken asshole keeled over next to this beat-to-shit garbage can finishes vomiting all over the sidewalk and looks up at me with glassy, reddened eyes. He mumbles something I can't understand, his slurred words sounding like some kind of extraterrestrial mating call.

I toss a dollar bill at the prick and compliment him on an impressive avant-garde busking routine. The narrator tells me that 'transgressive performance art' probably would've sounded better just as the boozehound collapses onto a sewer grate and howls an eclectic array of expletives into the crisp night air.

«««—»»»

Business is slow tonight. For the restaurant anyway.

A handful of bored-looking customers are scattered throughout a spacious dining area. Dozens of tables sit empty as I continue to linger near the main entrance, pretending to scribe a lengthy email or text message on my state-of-the-art smartphone.

Out of nowhere this clumsy, weird-looking busboy bumps into me. He apologizes. 'Profusely.' I don't say anything but give the guy a harsh look, like he's lucky to still be breathing after invading my personal space. He scurries off with his tail between his legs. I'm finally in character.

THE SPARTAK TRIGGER

The mark is sitting alone at the bar, just as he's been instructed to do. He looks nervous. Real nervous. I'm ten minutes late and he's checking his watch every twenty seconds or so, probably telling himself he'll get up and leave if I don't show up soon. But he won't leave. It's too much money. He'll sit there for an hour if I let him. Lucky for him I've got a plane to catch, another appointment to keep. I take a deep, easy breath and make my way over to the bar.

The mark is momentarily distracted by something and nearly falls off of his stool when I 'affably' slap him on the back. I say hello and swiftly situate myself upon the open seat next to him.

"Jesus!" he shouts, nearly spilling his cocktail. "You scared the hell out of me."

"Sorry I'm late." I help myself to a handful of peanuts from a cheap plastic bowl. The bartender asks me what I want and I tell him to grab me whatever beer in his fridge is the coldest. He nods and asks the mark if he'd like another seven and seven.

"Yeah," he says. "Make it a double."

As soon as the bartender's back is turned I reach into my overcoat and pull out a thickly-packed baronial envelope. I slide it along a surprisingly-glossy bar top towards the floor model businessman.

"What's that?" he asks, his voice trembling.

"Consider it a down payment." The peanuts are stale and I suddenly wish I'd picked a classier joint at which to ruin this assclown's life.

"Listen, I'm still not sure if I want to do this… I'm not even sure I *can* do it. I mean, my security clearance is still only at level five." The mark runs a recently-manicured hand through his thinning blonde hair, his 'countenance drowning in a pool of discomfort.'

"Come on now, I thought you were some kind of hot shot Vice President over there at Tetrace."

"Look, man, I'm just a junior V.P. okay—a fucking nobody in the grand scheme of things. There are a dozen or so senior V.P.'s above me, plus the president, the C.E.O., the C.F.O., the board of governors, and so on..." The mark's awkward anxiety is getting worse by the second, a light glaze now blanketing his dark, beady eyes. "I don't even know what I'm doing here."

I crack my knuckles. Purely for effect. I give the mark the look I gave the busboy earlier, just to let him know I'm not messing around. "You read a letter I sent you that promised you a shitload of money in exchange for betraying your employer and you're a greedy son of a bitch. That's what you're doing here, Daniels."

The mark glares at me strangely. He seems surprised that I know his name for some reason. The narrator quickly explains why I always set up these types of meetings by corresponding through the old-fashioned 'snail mail' system as our surly, beer-gutted bartender brings us the drinks we ordered. I toss a twenty at him and tell him to keep the change. He smiles widely, folding the bill in half and tucking it in his shirt pocket as he waddles back over to a poorly-mounted television set on the far side of the bar.

I lean in towards the mark, injecting a healthy dose of sternness into my 'sand paper voice.' "Listen, Daniels, your security level doesn't even matter. All my client needs you to do is copy and paste this file onto the desktop of any computer connected to the communal hard drive. That's it." I pull out a tiny flash disc drive and place it in front of him. "It's foolproof. You can do it from anywhere in the building. Piece of cake, alright?"

He looks at the disc like it's some kind of disease-infested dishrag. "Why me then, huh? Why don't you just get some entry-level programmer or an inside sales associate to do it?"

"Because all non-executives at Tetrace are inspected upon entering and exiting the building, you know that. Take the disc. Do the job. Take the money. Buy yourself a nice condo someplace tropical."

"Who's your client? Is it Bleep? It is, isn't it?"

"I'm not at liberty to divulge that information." I decide to start talking to the mark like he's a dimwitted schoolboy—a technique I used quite a bit on uncooperative gangbangers back when I was on the force.

THE SPARTAK TRIGGER

"Okay. Look. This is really simple, junior V.P. boy. Pick the disc up and put it in your pocket. When you go to work tomorrow morning, plug it into the data port on some seldom-used computer on the tenth floor, which is being renovated."

The mark's disposition swiftly graduates from restrained fear to outright alarm. His lower lip stops quivering and then begins to convulse wildly, like a trophy-sized trout being pulled into a rowboat. "H-H-How did you know about that?"

"It doesn't matter." I'm looking down at myself playing this character, the level of cool I'm radiating rapidly approaching absolute zero. "No one important will be around, just a few guys on the construction crew maybe. If someone you do know sees you just say you got off on the wrong floor by mistake, that you haven't had your triple tall mocha latte bullshit yet and that's made you disoriented. If you can't get it done in the morning, just sneak down at lunchtime. It'll take you five minutes tops. Two hundred grand per minute's a pretty decent wage the last time I checked."

Daniels clearly doesn't like being addressed in such a condescending manner. He's not afraid anymore, far from it. He now seems kind of pissed off that I would dare to talk to him like he's some kind of simpleton. Good. Fear is almost never productive. Anger is at least a facilitator for action in most situations.

So now this skinny Ivy League graduate is 'glowering' at me. Harshly. I get the sense he'd punch me in the face if he wasn't such a pampered weakling. That's exactly what he is though. That's exactly what all these guys are. He won't do a goddamn thing.

"And you're absolutely sure there's no way this will get back to me?" the mark asks.

I peel the label off of the glacier-cold beer bottle I ordered earlier, its contents still untouched. "Absolutely not. The virus is on a three-hour time-delay and will automatically wipe out any traces of when and where it's uploaded as soon as it's activated. Trust me. If you get busted it gets them one step closer to my client. Obviously that's something we'd like to avoid."

He takes the disc and the envelope, releasing a heavy sigh as he accepts that logic and tucks both items into his jacket pocket. "When do I get the rest of the money?"

I look around to give the impression that I'm concerned that someone might be watching us before responding in a 'hushed' tone. "There's ten grand in that envelope I just gave you. I'll transfer ninety more into your third party's offshore account later tonight. Have you got the routing digits?"

Daniels half-stands up and pulls a light blue index card out of his back pocket, clumsily handing it to me like a fourth-string quarterback nearly botching a basic run play. "And the rest of it?"

"The rest of the million will be automatically delivered as soon as Tetrace dot com goes offline. So. Do you understand completely what you're meant to do here, sport?"

Daniels nods reluctantly, wiping a shimmering sheet of sweat from his brow with a grimy bar napkin prior to guzzling the entirety of his drink in a single swig. It hasn't been one of my better performances but he seems to have bought it—hook, line, and sinker.

"Okay then." I stand up and straighten my overcoat. The mark refuses to acknowledge me. He's fixedly staring into the empty glass sitting in front of him.

"Aren't you going to drink your beer?" he asks, plainly.

"I'm not thirsty. It's been a pleasure doing business with you, Daniels. Enjoy the rest of your evening."

According to the narrator I'm 'bounding giddily' as I depart the scene but that sounds pretty fruity to me so let's just say I'm glad it went well. Once I'm a few blocks away from the restaurant I whip out my smartphone and text my boss a pair of asterisks, letting him know that he should go ahead and proceed with the phony wire transfer. He texts me back one of those stupid colon/bracket smiley face things. I send him the account number Daniels gave me and shut my zPhone down for the night.

The only thing that can screw things up now is if the mark tries to use any of the counterfeit bills I gave him later tonight.

THE SPARTAK TRIGGER

But that probably won't happen. I seriously doubt it anyway. You never know though. You can never be one hundred percent certain of anything after all, especially in situations such as these...

《《《—》》》

For some reason I'm trying to remember the combination to my high school gym locker as Leslie leads me up her shitty motel's uneven staircase. It used to be that when I visited this place it was to shake the proprietors down for a payout in exchange for me and my partner looking the other way. Then when Leslie took over she offered to pay us in contra and we didn't think twice about making a new arrangement with her. Now that I'm not a cop anymore I have to pay like everyone else which is kind of gay. It's not a big deal though since I'm making more money with Sancus than I ever did on the force, kickbacks included. So. Yeah.

We walk down the second floor corridor 'shrouded' in a strangely-comforting silence. Leslie's never really been much for chitchat, which has always been fine with me. I notice a few grey hairs sprouting from her scalp as I follow her. She must be getting up there age-wise, not that I'm getting any younger or anything. It's kind of weird I guess, knowing someone for ten or fifteen years and never saying more than a few sentences to them in total. Whatever.

Leslie stops at a door near the end of the hallway and opens it without knocking. I follow her inside and there are eight or nine decent-looking whores sitting around in a circle smoking. They stop talking as soon as Leslie walks in and it takes them just a few seconds to extinguish their cigarettes and stand up in a manner that effectively puts their best assets on display. The skinny girls bend over to flaunt their asses and the bigger girls lean forward to show off their cleavage.

I've always been a boob man myself so it doesn't take me long to make my choice and then a few minutes later I'm alone in a room with this broad named Sandra and she's rubbing my cock, trying to get me hard. It doesn't seem to be working. Fuck.

"Do you want to just talk for a bit and try again in a minute?" she asks, gently. Her luridly-applied makeup makes her look a lot older than she probably is. She's not quite pretty but not exactly ugly either. A look of 'sublime relief' is percolating behind her soft, hazel eyes.

"This has never happened to me," I lie.

"It's okay. Do you want me to leave and send one of the other girls back in?"

"No, that's okay. Let's just hang out for a bit, like you said."

"Okay."

She contorts herself into an odd-looking crouching position at the foot of the bed and her flabby stomach is oozing out of an exceedingly low-cut shirt. I try not to stare at the juicy flesh cluster but can't help myself.

"So, like, what do you do for a job, Mister?" she asks, 'good-humoredly.'

"I'm not allowed to talk about it, sorry."

"Sounds like interesting work."

"Yeah, I guess it is pretty interesting now that you mention it."

Sandra starts fiddling with her bleached blonde hair in a deliciously-childish manner. The narrator points out that this would normally turn me on but tonight it just frustrates me further.

I can't think of anything else to say and then I notice a look of pity making its way across Sandra's semi-attractive face. A 'searing humiliation' knifes through me as a tepid wave of blood rushes to my face, the wrong direction I want it to flow. I know full-well that this whole scene has been contrived by the narrator to make me seem like some kind of 'anti-archetype' or whatever but that doesn't make dealing with it any easier…

"So, yeah, are you, like, from Phoenix originally?" the whore asks.

"Listen, I don't think this is going to work out." I stand up and put my shirt back on as Sandra stumbles gracelessly off the bed.

THE SPARTAK TRIGGER

"Oh, um, okay. We've still got to charge you for the full hour though," she stammers, as if she's the one who's embarrassed now.
"That's fine. See you later."
"See you later."

⟪⟨⟨—⟩⟩⟫

My eyes are burning with exhaustion as I stagger into my boss' office, which is on the ground floor of an innocuous four-story building in this lame industrial park on the outskirts of Scottsdale. I'm fifteen minutes late for our meeting. Okay, twenty. I don't know why Dave wants to see me so friggin' early but I'm cursing myself for not rescheduling as I nearly spill my extra-large gas station coffee onto what has got to be a really good knockoff of a Persian rug.

Dave's secretary greets me with 'poorly-concealed contempt' as I make my entrance. "Good morning, Mister Bishop, please take a seat." Shelly used to be smoking hot but she's been packing on the pounds lately, probably from dealing with a breakup or an abortion or something. I'd still do her though. Totally.

Just as I'm getting ready to dissolve into one of the plush leather waiting room chairs Sancus, Inc. has recently invested in, Dave's voice comes booming over the intercom. He tells Shelly to send me in. She goes ahead and tells me that Mr. Baxter will see me now. I think about telling her that I'm not fucking deaf but then I don't.

I walk into the big man's office and he tries to stand up to greet me but the three hundred pounds he's carrying have other ideas. "Good to see you, Bish." I reach across his desk and shake his blubbery hand, meekly. He grunts and tells me to sit down. I oblige.

There's a new family portrait sitting on Dave's desk. His teenaged sons look completely disinterested in anything while his dwarfish wife smiles enigmatically at the department store camera lens. Dave catches me looking at the photo and I think for a second he might give me an unsolicited update on how Mary, Todd and Joey are doing but instead he offers me a cigar that one of his other agents brought back from a vacation in Havana. "I don't smoke those things," I say. "Thanks though."

"Me neither. I'm not sure why Viper gave them to me to be honest. I would've preferred a nice bottle of rum or something. Anyway. Let's have a look at the Tetrace file then, shall we?"

"Yup, sounds good." I start to feel a bit anxious which the narrator thinks might have something to do the fact that I've never really been comfortable with the whole boss/employee dynamic. Lucky guess.

Dave puts the box of cigars away and pulls out a manila file folder. The narrator mentions that the tattered salt-and-pepper beard blanketing his plump face looks like it's about due for a fresh dye job which feels like gratuitous information but I suppose there could be a reason for it. Stay tuned. Dave leafs through the folder for a few seconds, closely inspecting each page with the perverse precision of a celibate gynecologist.

"Okay, so… I actually just got off the phone with my contact at Tetrace right before you came in." My boss looks up from his folder at an unflattering angle that makes the dark circles under his greyish eyes appear more prominent than usual. "They caught Daniels trying to upload the file you gave him first thing this morning. Apparently the bastard cried like a baby when they canned him."

"That's a damn shame." We share a brief, not-quite-genuine laugh and I feel a lot better, the light anxiety I'd felt earlier now gone completely. FYI.

"That's the fifth exec they've had us go after in the last six months," I say, matter-of-factly. "They must have a paranoid board of directors over there."

"Yeah, probably something like that." I can tell that Dave knows the real reason Tetrace has been giving us so much business lately but he obviously doesn't want to fill me in on the details. Whatever. "I guess it doesn't matter as long as their checks keep clearing," Dave adds, triumphantly. "Speaking of which, here's your cut on the Daniels assignment." He hands me a thin envelope that I snatch greedily and store inside my shirt pocket.

"Thanks."

"No, thank you, Bish. By the way, I've got another job that just came across the wire this morning. Merlin was supposed to take it but he's got the flu or some shit. You think you can handle another assignment this week?"

I usually like to take a few days off between jobs but I'm in a good mood and could use the cash. "Yeah, sure, no problem." I affect an air of heroism, like I'm a government assassin being charged with taking out an evil South American dictator or something. "What's the job? Another high-tech corporate monkey with a super-expensive severance package?"

"Naw, this one works for a big investment firm up in Seattle." Dave cracks his knuckles, loudly. "Company's called Silverman Chase. You've probably heard of it."

Nope. "Nope."

"Well, anyway, they want to get rid of this dame but they can't just fire her for some reason." Dave slides a single sheet of paper towards me, a color photograph of a decent-looking cougar titivating its top right corner. "She probably blew the C.E.O. and they're worried about a lawsuit."

"I'd take a gummer from this slut," I offer.

"Yeah, well, if you pull this job off she'll probably be reduced to turning tricks on some street corner soon enough." A broad, mischievous smile engraves itself upon Dave's ruddy face with the slow, deliberate pacing of a master craftsman. "After doing some time for possession that is."

"Ah, so we're pulling a triple-S on this one, huh? Stealth Snow Storm."

"Exactly. Everything you need to know is all in here." He tosses a big white envelope at me and I fumble with it for a second or two before it hits the ground.

"Christ!" Dave exclaims. "I thought you said you played tight end at State."

"That was a long time ago." I pick the envelope up off the floor and start to open it before Dave tells me to stop.

"I've got another appointment right now, Bish," he says. "You can look through that at home, it's just the mark's itinerary and whatnot. They want this done by Friday though, is that good with you?"

"Hey, you're the boss. I'll take care of it, no problem." We shake hands and I leave. I make a pass at Shelly on my way out of the office. She tells me to go to hell. Bitch.

«««—»»»

I order a crispy chicken combo from this retarded-looking black teenager whose greasy-stained uniform is all disheveled and gross. The total comes to $8.55 but the kid doesn't give me any change after I hand him a ten and then he acts like he's distracted by something and starts pretending he's really busy and shit. I know full fucking well what he's doing but I'm tired and don't really feel like getting into a fight with some idiot over $1.45.

It takes forever for them to get my order processed and then I'm eating my sandwich in my car and cutting off every black driver I can find on the highway. When I'm finally alone in my apartment I rip open the warm paper bag to get my fries and then it hits me—I never asked for any ketchup. Fuck.

«««—»»»

The airport's undergoing some major renovations so every line-up is a lot longer than normal. Luckily all I've got with me is a perfectly-sized carry-on bag so I don't need to check any luggage in. Boo-yah.

Some cunt in one of the Dakotas was busted trying to smuggle some nitroglycerine onto a flight last week so security's pretty tight and they give each and every passenger a thorough once-over after they pass through the metal detector. The punk at my station gives me a look like he knows me and doesn't like me. He makes me take my shoes off. I hand over my black oxfords and he scampers off to some top secret shoe inspection booth somewhere. The narrator mentions the guy's tiny wrist tattoo as he's describing him to us and then I think maybe I arrested him or something back in the day. *Former gang member?* No. That's not it. I know him from somewhere else.

I sit sock-footed at the security station for ten minutes and then fifteen. The 'tetchy' security agent who took my shoes finally comes back and tells me to follow him. I ask where my shoes are and he ignores me.

The guy's face is really starting to look familiar to me then and I realize that he dated my daughter a long time ago, back when she was in high school. *He's the kid you caught sneaking into Iris' room and bashed the shit out of with a crowbar. The big baseball star.*

We walk into a small, formal-looking room and he tells me to take a seat. "What's this all about?" I ask, slightly more forcefully than I'd planned.

"Take a seat, Mr. Bishop."

"Alright." I lower myself onto a hard wooden chair. "How's your arm by the way?"

"I never pitched again, thanks for asking."

My daughter's ex leaves the room and no one else comes to see me so I just get up and walk out. I buy a new pair of shoes at a discount men's fashion kiosk and get to my gate just as they're announcing the final boarding call for Flight 24601 with service to Seattle.

«‹‹—››»

The cheapest motel I can find in the Emerald City is in a rundown part of town and the clerk sizes me up like I'm a fugitive arms dealer or something when he hands me my room key.

I give the old bastard a dirty look and spit on the floor, just to see what he'll do. He just laughs and lights a cigarette.

I flip through the phone book in my room after taking a quick shower. There's only one comedy club on this side of town and when I call them up it takes ten fucking rings for someone to answer.

"Hello?" some high-voiced moron squeals into my ear.

"Yeah, hey, is it amateur night there tonight by any chance?"

"Indeed it is. We're open 'til one."

He slams the phone down and I think of all kinds of awful things I might do to the cocksucker when I see him but then I calm down using a breathing technique this androgynous police therapist taught me once.

I walk into Chuckle Central and grab a spot at the bar. Some twenty-something loser in glasses and a cardigan is on stage whining about grad school. His latest punch line is something about existential hair dressers only using post-modern conditioner. His delivery is all slow-paced and morose, his body language acutely meek.

A harsh, telling silence floods the room.

He keeps going for some reason and it's like watching a mortally-wounded animal struggle to get across the interstate. "Right…and I also just invented a video game console for the terminally bored… It's called an en-wii… An en-wii."

A smattering of reluctant giggles is the best a meager crowd can offer.

"Um, so, yeah. So, also, I finally finished my senior thesis the other day." The liberal arts douchebag starts fiddling arbitrarily with his glasses. "Um, my major was Graphic Irony…and the paper was on sodomy with a plunger! Thanks very much folks, you've, um, been a terrific audience, really terrific, thanks."

A few people in the mood for charity offer a half-hearted, sympathetic applause. A few more boo. I just stand there and watch

THE SPARTAK TRIGGER

him sulk off of the stage, taking a generous helping from the Schadenfreude Buffet as the wannabe comedian fights off tears.

Some doughy, spiky-haired faggot wearing a Hawaiian shirt ambles on stage and sarcastically thanks the kid for coming out. Aloha Man plugs the ultra-hip FM radio station he works for before inviting the next amateur on stage.

A lanky guy—handsome, mid-thirties—jumps out from behind a maroon curtain and a table of friends gives him a standing ovation as he makes his way up to the microphone and introduces himself as Dickie Gunn. He's blatantly wired, fervently scratching his nose every few seconds. I lean back and breathe easy now that I've got what I came for.

The drug-fuelled-comic races through several off-color jokes, at one point advising the crowd that it doesn't matter how much protection or birth control you use—knocking boots in a pterodactyl's nest just can't be considered *safe sex*. I catch myself laughing at this one and I almost decide to pick someone else but then I realize that it's late and I'm getting tired so I get ready to make my move.

Dickie's big finale is about how lepers must have to be really careful when they masturbate. He mimes an exaggeratedly-slow jerk-off motion while making some over-the-top facial expressions that are actually pretty hilarious. I applaud rigorously along with everyone else when he's done.

As soon as the radio DJ reappears I make my way over to the side of the stage and introduce myself to Dickie as a talent scout for a new cable channel called LaughTV that will show stand-up comics 24-hours-a-day. "We're looking for some fresh, up-and-coming acts right now," I say. Dickie's eyes light up like a flash inferno. He snatches a fake business card out of my hand and studies it like it's a successful alchemy formula or something.

"Can we step outside for a minute to talk?" I ask.

"Absolutely!" Dickie gives an enthusiastic thumbs-up to the table of sycophantic dickheads he's brought with him and we make our way out onto the street. I offer him a cigarette and he tells me he doesn't smoke. I tell him I don't either and then my right fist slams into his sternum in a firm, precise strike that knocks the funnyman on his ass.

Dickie calls me a motherfucker while he's writhing in agony on the sidewalk. I reach into his jacket pocket and pull out a clear plastic bag that's half-filled with white powder. He makes no effort to stop me.

"You've got talent, bud. Stick with it." I walk away just as a few club patrons show up and ask Dickie if he's okay. I'll be long gone by the time he manages to explain it to them.

«‹‹—›››

When I get back to the motel I take out the baggie I swiped from Dickie and hold it up for inspection against my bedside lamp. It's not a ton of coke, maybe five or six grams. It's more than enough for what I need it for though, plenty to spare even. I help myself to a couple of lines and then call the front desk to ask the 'curmudgeonly' clerk if he'll order me in an inexpensive hooker.

He tells me he'll see what he can do. I tell him that's not good enough and make some pretty graphic threats that he seems unresponsive to. The river of anger surging through me is pretty intense and I must pass out from it because the next thing I know the sun's up and I'm lying face down on the floor. My spine is killing me and the back of my head's really sore for some reason.

«‹‹—›››

According to the information I've been given, Olivia Jennings arrives at the office every day at exactly 8:15 A.M. and takes her lunch break right at noon. Her coworkers are all long gone by the time she heads back to her condo at quarter-past eight at night. Total workaholic. She won't know what to do with herself sans career.

THE SPARTAK TRIGGER

Silverman Chase's corporate headquarters are incredibly tacky. A bright neon sign flaunting their gaudy logo adorns the central facade. The rest of the building's normal-looking enough I guess, nothing too spectacular. Their windows are all polished and everything but the sign's just too much. It ruins the whole thing, aesthetically-speaking at least.

I'm sitting in my rental car across the street from the company's employee parking lot, watching the tinted-glass entrance through a pair of high-tech binoculars that Dave hooked me up with back when I first started at Sancus. Finance dork after finance dork walks in and out, the only broads I see chubby secretary-types that I wouldn't even stick the narrator's tiny dick in.

Finally, right at noon, a pair of long, shapely legs emerge that my eyes 'follow with approval' up to a firm, taut body that oozes pure sexuality. It takes me a few seconds to reach this chick's face and then I realize that it's the mark. She's a lot hotter than her picture suggested she'd be. A company head shot doesn't really offer much in the way of cleavage measurements and such though. Too bad.

I watch Jennings get into a blue, European-made sedan and then I fire up my coupe. She drives to an out-of-the-way diner and I'm three car lengths behind her the entire trip. When she leaves her sedan to go eat I grab what's left of Dickie's blow and enter the grimy restaurant a minute or so behind her. The narrator goes into excessive detail in describing this greasy spoon we're at, telling us about all the photos and paraphernalia on the walls and shit. I just tune him out and focus on the job at hand.

When I walk past Jennings' booth she catches me ogling her and gives me a look of disgust meant to embarrass me. But it doesn't. Not even close. She's probably given that look to hundreds of dirt bags like me over the years. God knows I've received my fair share of looks like that from women like this.

I grab a spot at the counter a few yards from where the mark is sitting and I order a club sandwich. I overhear Jennings ask for a garden salad and an ice water. The guy sitting next to me is wearing overalls and talking to himself about diesel engines. Our homely waitress eventually puts a cheeseburger platter in front of him and that shuts him up.

After a few minutes Jennings gets up to use the restroom and I stare at her luscious ass while she struts sensually across the diner's creaky floorboards. A moment later she's walking back towards her booth and I swiftly exit my stool. On my way to the men's room I bump into her and covertly drop the bag of coke into her open purse. I tell her I'm sorry and she calls me an asshole. Lovely.

There's a payphone right by the bathrooms and I use it to call the cops and leave an anonymous tip. I get my club sandwich to go and a squad car arrives just as I'm leaving for the airport.

The river card's the three of hearts and that puts a possible flush in play. I look down at my pocket kings just as Roger pushes all of his chips into the middle of the table. The guy sitting next to me folds and I count my stack to see if I've got the bet covered. Not quite.

Roger's giving me a cockeyed look and I know I'm not going to get an earnest read off of him so I muck my hand and tell him to take it down.

"Good fold," he tells me, pulling a couple hundred bucks worth of chips towards him. A sly grin struts across his pale, angular face and a pair of bushy black eyebrows elevate to form an expression of 'brazen arrogance.' Bastard.

It's three in the morning and we've been playing for six hours but no one's really taken a stranglehold of the game. Usually by now either me or Roger's made use of our finely-honed skills and seized control of the chip lead but tonight Derek and his semi-mute buddy who I think said he's from Mesa have managed to hang in with us. Good for them.

We spent the first couple hours of the evening exchanging aggrandized tales about our various sexual conquests but the last dozen or so hands have been played inside a conversational vacuum. Whatever.

"You guys ever play cards online?" Derek asks us out of nowhere, the wad of tobacco jammed in his mouth making his words difficult to make out. "I play at Poker Nation sometimes, it's actually kinda fun."

There's a few seconds of coarse-tinged silence before someone responds.

"I don't," Roger states icily as he diligently shuffles the cards. "And I'll bet dollars to donuts that my old partner over there doesn't either." I hate that he still knows me so well, especially since we haven't spent a whole lot of time together these last few years. It's like I haven't changed at all since we were on the force together which is true I guess but hard to accept for some reason.

"Is he right?" Derek cuts the deck, giving us a generous whiff of Blue Collar Body Odor cologne when he lifts his arm.

"Yeah, he's right." The dealer fires two cards at me face down. "Never much got the point of that internet poker junk to be honest. I mean, it's like watching porn instead of getting laid, y'know?"

"Speaking of online bullshit, any of you guys ever tried online dating?" the guy sitting next to me whose name I can't remember asks us.

"Yeah, I was a member of that Love Connection site for a few months last year," Derek instantly moans. "Not a great experience." The narrator talks over him as he tells the rest of his stupid story. He explains to us that the dozen-odd ladies Derek chatted with through the site all posted favorable photos of themselves that were taken from angles that made them look attractive and thin but then when he met them in person they all turned out to be ugly porkers. He tried to delete his account a few times but their exit page used really hard-to-understand language and they kept tricking him into retaining his subscription, a fact Derek himself relates to us just as the narrator's account of the enthralling saga ends. "Eventually I had to cancel my credit card to get out of it."

The narrator keeps going and eventually makes a snide comment about how online dating's rising popularity is dangerous in the long-term since it reduces our personalities into 'inane tidbits from which profound consequences are extrapolated' and that somehow trivializes the most vital elements of humanity. I don't really get what he's trying to say and I'm pretty sure he doesn't either.

"Fascinating, D-Train, just fascinating." I look down at my cards and see the seven of clubs and the two of spades. Mathematically speaking it's the worst hand possible. Derek's first to act and he folds. John Doe does the same. I'm the small blind and I think about mucking but then I decide to make a small raise after catching Roger stroking his chin—an old tell he sometimes forgets to suppress.

Roger waits a minute before re-raising and then I go all in without hesitation and he tosses his hand into the middle of the table a few seconds later. "You can have it," he snarls.

I tell Roger he made a bad fold and a look of anguish invades his eyes as he realizes that I was bluffing. I guess he doesn't know me as well as we thought.

«««—»»»

Dave doesn't look at all healthy. He's morbidly obese, sure, but that doesn't explain the jaundiced skin, puffy eyes, or pallid complexion he's rockin' today. I hope I don't catch whatever the hell he's got as I sit there waiting for him to talk. Good times.

"You're on a real hot streak, Bish," Dave tells me, like I don't already know. "The Jennings termination went smooth as all get out from what I heard. She freaked out when the cops showed up and they charged her with resisting arrest in addition to narcotics possession. Her contract at Silverman Chase is now completely null and void. Nice and clean."

"Awesome." I'm running on two hours' sleep and everything seems like its in slow motion, shot through a Rotoscope lens.

THE SPARTAK TRIGGER

"So our good friends at Tetrace gave me a call this morning." Dave's decided to raise his voice for some reason. "Apparently they're in the final stages of acquiring ChumSpot and, on top of getting the lion's share of the buyout profits, their acting C.E.O. managed to retain his inflated salary and benefits and junk as part of the deal."

"What's ChumSpot?" I know full-well what it is but I want Dave to explain it to you (even though it's a pretty obvious pastiche) instead of the narrator, who starts grumbling about my bad attitude but then the editor tells him he's used way too many ellipses thus far so he goes back and starts taking a bunch of them out of the text. Cool.

"It's this big social networking website." Dave sneezes and waits for me to say 'bless you' or 'gesundheit' but I say 'deiseal' instead since I just read somewhere that that's the response the Gaels use and I'm part-Irish so…yeah. My boss looks confused for a second but then shakes it off and continues talking about ChumSpot: "It started out as a college campus thing but then it went mainstream and took off like crazy. They've got something like a hundred gazillion subscribers now."

The color is starting to return to Dave's face but he still looks quite ill and I'm worried he might keel over and die at any minute and completely ruin my day. He has a pretty gross cough attack and then he smashes a pudgy paw down on his intercom and tells Shelly to bring him some water. She immediately strolls in and hands him a bottle of some expensive imported shit. She catches me checking out her awesome tits and then 'scowls harshly' at the flirtatious smile I give her.

Shelly leaves without saying a word to either of us but I'm not sure Dave even noticed. The big guy pounds back a few gulps of luxury water and continues: "So, bottom line, they want this fucker gone completely and they want *us* to make sure he violates a very specific clause in his contract pertaining to arrests that would be deemed damaging to the company's image and reputation. They want something public, something headline-worthy but not narcotics possession. Got it?"

This is a new one. "This is a new one."

"Yeah, we're gonna have to get creative here, Bish. You could try liquoring him up and get him busted for drunk and disorderly conduct or maybe pants him and have him busted for indecent exposure. I don't know, what do you think?"

I look out the window behind Dave's majestic leather throne chair and stare at the ocean of sand and cacti that stretches out for eternity beyond a row of metallic garbage bins. My brow's been furrowed to make it seem like I'm trying to come up with a solution to the problem at hand but all I'm really doing right now is trying to stay awake. Dave keeps looking at me, waiting for me to say something. I acquiesce after taking a deep, theatrical breath. "This is a tough one, Boss."

Tiny beads of perspiration are oozing out of Dave's forehead and I watch them trickle down towards his offset eyes as he sits staring at me, thinking I've got something else to add. Then out of nowhere I remember a story I saw on the news about a guy who went on a rampage at a mini-mall down in Tucson last month. He was wired on synthetic adrenaline and went berserk when the rent-a-cops tried to get him to stop harassing women in the food court. They needed like a half-dozen taser blasts to take him down and he ended up spending a week in the hospital. The hot Middle Eastern broad who covered the story said a bunch of lawsuits are in the works at the end of her report.

I announce to Dave that I've got an idea and his 'grotesquely-porcine' face flushes with excitement as he leans forward and asks me what it is.

"Well I could probably figure out a way to give this ChumSpot guy a shot of this stuff called 'epinephrine.' I saw a thing about it on the news—kids take it and it gets them all wired up and they go completely crazy, bonkers".

Dave's grinning and I can tell he likes what he hears.

"So, yeah, I could give him that, maybe drop it in his coffee…" I can't fight off a yawn. "…and then set up a scenario where he'll freak out on someone. Maybe get him to road rage at a busy intersection or something. That should do the trick I guess."

Dave slams his fat hand down on the table again, just missing the intercom. "Brilliant!" His beefy jowls gyrate like a free-standing gelatin dessert stationed in the buffet cart of an undulating passenger train. *What?*

"I know a guy up in Flagstaff who can get us any chemical we need so let me handle that part." Dave grabs a pen and a notepad from his top drawer. "You say this stuff's called 'epinephrine'?" I nod and he scribbles down a note that looks like some kind of ancient Chinese chicken scratch.

"What's the timeline on this one by the way?" I ask. The narrator tells me I'm 'beaming with professional zeal' as my eyelids' heftiness continues unabated.

"That's the good news," Dave says. "They aren't going public with the deal until next month so you've got a lot of time to play with."

"That's not necessarily a good thing," I tell him. "Where's this ChumSpot guy located anyway?"

"San Diego." Dave wipes his runny nose with a souvenir napkin procured from a regional fast food chain. "Maybe you can squeeze in a trip to the zoo while you're out there."

"Yeah. Maybe." I fucking hate zoos.

«««—»»»

There's nothing good on TV tonight and I can't get a game anywhere so I decide to try out the online poker site Derek told me about. My computer's not the best in the league but I'm pretty sure it can handle the workload.

I log onto PokerNation.com and create an account. All of the good usernames are taken it seems. Somebody's already got PocketAces, AceInTheHole, StraightFlush, Str8Flush, CardShark, GreatWhite, Gr8White, TrumpCard, etc. I eventually just go with 00ShaneBish_60 and punch in my credit card number. I get a hundred bucks worth of chips and head over to a pot limit game of virtual Omaha hold 'em.

GreatWhite is at my table and I automatically hate him. When he gets knocked out on the first hand I sit in on I pray to god that he kills himself or at least deletes his account so I can get the username.

The cartoon dealer keeps giving me rags and I'm starting to get mad. I finally get a decent hand after like an hour and make a healthy bet that everyone at my table calls me on. I end up losing and my computer monitor takes the business end of a nine iron like a champ.

«««—»»»

I'm reading a sports magazine in our preferred airline's second-rate frequent flyers lounge and a guy sits down next to me that I recognize from a semi-recent assignment. He didn't take the bait so I assume he received the career advancement whatever company he's with was considering him for.

"Congratulations on the promotion," I tell him without looking up from my magazine.

"Thanks…do I know you?"

"No. And you're lucky that you don't."

The guy stands back up and walks out of the lounge, hurriedly.

«««—»»»

My motel's out in the middle of nowhere and the in-house bar is closed by the time I check in. Fuck.

I channel surf for a long time and finally start watching a popular sketch comedy show that's pretty funny once in a while. They air a decent skit about a human resources coordinator who gets summoned into his boss' office to get chewed out about harassing his coworkers because he's incorrectly assumed he has immunity against stuff like that because he's the one they're supposed to register complaints with. The studio audience doesn't give the well-written sequence the credit it deserves.

When the sketch is over a commercial airs promoting a revolutionary new home cleaning product and the super-hyper pitchman—who I'm pretty sure died recently—is going bananas talking about how awesome this stuff is. My apartment back home is pretty friggin' dirty so I call the toll-free number on my zPhone and order a case of the stuff before the ten minute window during which you get a second case for free expires. Boom.

Twenty minutes later some Hispanic-sounding bitch at a telemarketing company calls me up and congratulates me on my recent purchase of OMNI-CLEAN. She tells me that it's my lucky day and that she's been authorized to offer me $100 in free gas vouchers if I sign up for the Super Budget Discount Rewards Club at their introductory rate of only five dollars per month. The fast-talking dame gets through about eight sentences before taking a breath, giving me no chance whatsoever to interrupt her. She finally asks me if I'd like to take advantage of this amazing offer and I tell her no and hang up.

An hour later some other slut calls trying to sell me the same bullshit and I pretend to have downs syndrome for a while until she gets frustrated and hangs up on me. Delicious.

«««—»»»

The midday San Diego sun is insanely powerful and I'm sweating buckets in my rental car even with the shitty air conditioning system cranked up full blast.

While I'm waiting for the mark to appear I log onto ChumSpot.com on my smartphone and set up a fake profile for the alias I used to use in my undercover cop days: Kyle Johnson. I plug in all of Kyle's fake information and then search for chums to add. It all seems pretty ridiculous but most things seem that way to me nowadays.

I find my daughter's profile after weeding through a few other Iris Bishops and send her a chum request. She looks happy in her profile photo. I try to remember the last time I talked to her and can't. It's been at least a couple of years I guess. *Deborah's funeral? Naw, can't be... Well, maybe.*

A large group of overexcited yuppies is meandering out of ChumSpot's main entrance, all of them dressed in expensive-looking clothes. I look down at the photo Dave gave me and then back up at the cluster of ChumSpot employees, confirming that the mark is not amongst them. I turn my attention back to my zPhone but the battery's dead or something and the screen's totally blank. Fuck.

The mark doesn't show up for work until late in the afternoon and he's got a woman with him that's remarkably plain-looking. They only spend a few minutes in the building and then they look as if they're having an intense argument on their way back to the super-rich nerd's exotic convertible.

I fire up the foreign station wagon Shelly arranged for me and get ready to trail ChumSpot's founder and C.E.O. for a bit when I hear two deafening gunshots ring out. I instinctively cower like a little bitch, throwing my arms over my head and crouching down low.

After the initial shock wears off I gather my senses and look back out the driver's side window. I don't need my binoculars to see the mark lying on the ground in a pool of blood. His woman is screaming for help at the top of her lungs. The narrator skillfully conveys the surreal sense of delirium affronting the scene as I drive away, fast.

«««—»»»

I've left five messages on Dave's voicemail and the breathing technique I normally use to calm myself down isn't working. The walls in my tiny motel room are closing in on me and the narrator declares that 'a blanket of unease' is smothering me as I continue to pace back and forth across a cheap beige carpet.

THE SPARTAK TRIGGER

The shooting at ChumSpot's corporate headquarters is all over the news and I'm losing my mind trying to figure out what my next move should be. *This is fucked. The whole situation is absolutely fucked.*

My memory banks take me back to the first time I saw a dead body, during my first year on the force. This was during a particularly bad Chicano gang war in a part of town that Roger and I were charged with patrolling. The kid was only sixteen and we had to tell his parents, who thought it was our fault for some reason. The father did a year upstate after taking a swing at Roger as I recall.

At long last my smartphone starts to vibrate but when I answer it's not Dave's voice that I hear. Fuck. After we exchange passwords another agent from Sancus whose codename I only faintly recognize is telling me through a cheap-sounding digital distortion device that a suspicious fire at McCord Industrial Park has left us without an employer. Dave and Shelly are both dead.

«««—»»»

The elderly woman sitting next to me on the flight back to Phoenix is incredibly rude. She keeps bothering the stewardess for this and that and I finally tell her that we're not at a goddamn resort restaurant and she tells me to mind my own business. I call her a useless cow and she immediately begins to sob. She pages the stewardess yet again and politely asks if she can find someone on the flight for her to trade seats with.

«««—»»»

As soon as we land at Sky Harbor I can sense that something's amiss. My suspicions are confirmed when a pair of large men claiming to be federal agents accost me right when I walk into the main terminal. Their identification looks legit and I'm in no mood to make a scene so I just follow them out to their black minivan without saying a word.

When I get in the backseat of their tinted soccer-mom-mobile one of them throws a blindfold at me and tells me to put it on. I protest and ask them who the hell they really are just as they simultaneously bust out a pair of identical CZ-75 automatics. *Czech-made guns. No way in hell these guys are feds.* I put the blindfold on. One of them leans towards me and makes sure it's sufficiently snug. "Good job," he says.

We drive for what seems like an eternity before they let me remove my blindfold. Once it's off I look around and see that we're in the middle of the desert, no signs of civilization anywhere.

My stoic, muscle-bound captors talk briefly about football and I mention that I used to play for the Sun Devils. The one sitting in the passenger seat looks back at me with a sardonic grin emblazoned upon a stretch of facial real estate located directly north of a badly-scarred, protruding chin. He succinctly recaps my unimpressive career statistics: two catches, nine yards, one fumble.

"Yeah, and how many yards did you gain playing college ball, tough guy?" I try to sound assertive but the narrator uses a much different adjective to describe my delivery of the line. Whatever.

<<<—>>>

We finally stop at a random spot somewhere along the endless unpaved road we've been traveling down for at least an hour. My abductors get out and tell me to stay put. They leave me all alone in the van for a few minutes. I think about getting out and running but then I realize I don't know where the hell I am, plus we're in the fucking Arizona badlands. I wouldn't make it far before dehydration and exhaustion took turns sodomizing me.

A new, much older man opens the front door of the van and coolly slides into the driver's seat. He turns to face me. An unkempt mop of white hair is perched atop a leathery mug that looks like it was recently refurbished by a second-rate saddle maker at some Old West Frontier theme park. Despite his overly-bronzed skin this guy nonetheless radiates an austere, almost regal quality, as if he's just graduated from a 19th century finishing school over in England. He smiles 'salaciously' to reveal a set of impossibly white teeth.

My skin's tingling with discomfort as he introduces himself as Special Agent Jonathan Holbrook. He proceeds to explain that he's been investigating Sancus, Inc. for several months now as part of a covert government probe spearheaded by an agency he says I've never heard of and which doesn't officially exist. Real cloak-and-dagger shit here, people. I solemnly nod at the guy for a while, unsure of what to say or do.

After hastily complimenting me on my choice of footwear he casually mentions that the fire that killed my boss and his secretary has officially been classified as arson. He takes a moment to gauge my reaction which is stolid as fuck. Then the narrator says something that lets us know that, even if Holbrook is who he says he is, this discussion is violating all kinds of protocols and regulations and that I'm not going to be formally charged with anything today. This gives our conversation an abstract levity which is oddly comforting.

Holbrook seems to know my whole life story up until I left the force. He begins recounting it from memory with alarming accuracy, at one point pausing and asking me how Dave had gone about recruiting me into his company exactly. I dance around the question and tell him I only occasionally freelance with Sancus, which the narrator explains was originally incorporated as a private security firm. I reach for my license but Holbrook tells me not to bother. Then I tell him that I make my living largely as a professional poker player and he kind of snickers but then he sees that I'm somewhat serious and readopts a 'pretense of formality.'

The douchebag asks me what I was doing in San Diego and I tell him that I was sightseeing. I'm doing my best to broadcast an air of nonchalance, using some tricks I learned at an acting class the force had me take a while back to help me with my undercover work. Holbrook doesn't seem to be buying it though.

"Have you also been to Denver recently?" he asks, smugly. The boiling blood surging through my veins gets a few degrees hotter.

"Maybe. Why?"

"Well, there was a young executive at Tetrace that was recently terminated for trying to upload a virus onto the company's mainframe. He took his own life two days later, blew his brains out with a hunting rifle. You know anything about that, Bishop?"

After choking down what the narrator refers to as 'volcanic bemusement' I tell Holbrook that I haven't seen anything about that on the news. Then he asks me if I've ever made it up to Seattle and when I don't answer he tells me in his satin scepter voice that the mangled corpse of former Silverman Chase employee Olivia Jennings was found in the back of an abandoned roadster 72 hours after she was arrested for cocaine possession. I stop trying to act cool.

"Cancer stick?" Holbrook offers, holding up a bright blue pack of cigarettes. I nod and reach forward, my right hand shaking uncontrollably.

<<<——>>>

Holbrook's goons drop me off right in front of my building. They remind me that their boss' generous offer to help them round up my fellow Sancus agents and testify against them in exchange for leniency when I'm formally charged with conspiracy to commit murder is only good for another day but they don't leave me with any way to get in touch with them. Curious. Curious indeed.

I nearly vomit into my kitchen sink as soon as I enter my apartment, a 'barbarous vertigo' pillaging my central nervous system. *This is insane. This is all insane.*

THE SPARTAK TRIGGER

Holbrook seriously seems to believe that Dave was running an assassin-for-hire operation and that I'm somehow responsible for several suspicious deaths currently being investigated by the authorities, including the now-infamous murder of ChumSpot founder and C.E.O. Elliot Zimmerman. I didn't bother trying to explain to him what Sancus really did because that somehow sounded worse than murder at the time.

The narrator proclaims that I'm 'brooding with fiery angst, every fiber of my being awash in worriment.' I grimace at the shade of purple his prose just turned. It's embarrassing for both of us really.

I guess I should probably be focused on trying to figure out who the hell Holbrook really works for right now. I should definitely be worried about what the hell happened to Dave and Shelly. I should be utterly disturbed by the fact that I'm potentially about to become the prime suspect in a high-profile murder investigation. But I don't care about any of that. There's only one thing on my mind. *Run. While you still can.*

I decide I should flee to Mexico. Seems like that's the place fugitives always run to, right? I don't own many possessions that actually matter so I've got everything I need or want crammed into a single suitcase within fifteen minutes and I'm ready to get the hell out of dodge. Adios la vida.

«««—»»»

After getting as much money as I can out of an ATM I head to the only place I can think of that's even remotely safe right now—Leslie's brothel. She's surprised to see me since I hadn't made an appointment but when I hand her two hundred bucks cash she quickly escorts me into their new VIP Lounge.

I tell Leslie just wanna hang out for a few hours and she leaves me alone in the surprisingly-nice room. I collapse into a cloth-covered recliner and breathe for what feels like the first time in days. My brain won't let me stop planning though, not even for a moment. I haven't got enough cash to set up shop in Mexico yet but I've got sixty grand sitting in a safety deposit box at a bank in Glendale that will get me out of the country in style. I just need to grab that first thing in the morning and then I'm history. The narrator facetiously thanks me for being so forthright with the audience and I tell him to fuck off. Dick.

Some other asshole comes into the lounge. I tell him to leave me alone too and he scuttles off like his dick is bleeding. Leslie shows up two minutes later and gives me shit about it but I slip her another hundred and tell her to just make sure no one bothers me until morning.

"Do you want a room then?" she asks, her cadence almost motherly. It's a weird turn-on and I suddenly realize there *is* a way to get my troubles off my mind for a little while.

"Yeah, I guess that'd make more sense than hanging out in here. Might as well grab me one of your girls too. Not that Sandra bitch though."

«‹‹—›››

The room is hot when I wake up, a bright sun beaming through a large, uncovered window. I'm pretty groggy and it takes me a few minutes to find my smartphone. I turn it on and see that it's almost noon. Fuck. I guess I should've arranged for a wakeup call or something. I gather my shit and get ready to head over to the bank.

Leslie offers me a cup of coffee on my way out and I end up spending a few minutes sitting with her in the makeshift motel's tiny kitchenette. It turns out we went to the same high school a few years apart and she was once engaged to a distant cousin of mine. Small world. Our conversation relaxes me greatly and I almost forget that I have a government spook after me, that my boss was just murdered by an arsonist, and at any moment I could be arrested for a very serious crime. Almost. I thank Leslie for the coffee when I leave and she asks me when I'll be back.

"I don't know. I'm going out of town for a while"

"Well, have a good trip then." A playful, flirty look in Leslie's deep blue eyes makes her seem ten years younger. I think I'm blushing as I say goodbye and tell her to take care of herself.

I walk out of the brothel's front door and out of the corner of my eye I spot a black mini-van a block away from where my car is parked. My chest tightens as I take a few steps backwards, trying to figure out how the hell Holbrook's goons found me here.

«««—»»»

I take the long route to out to Glendale, the old highway my father helped build way back in the day. The black mini-van follows me closely, seemingly unconcerned with keeping their presence a secret. Holbrook's sending me a message. He can find me any time he wants. So he thinks at least.

My appearance must be a lot seedier than I realize because the bank teller goes to get her manager as soon as I tell her that the brass key I've brought with me is for a safety deposit box in their vault. I catch a glimpse of myself in a freshly-polished glass door and indeed see an ugly, disheveled, middle-aged stranger staring back at me. Whatever.

After standing around for a few minutes this impish Chinaman in a glossy silver suit appears out of nowhere and asks me if he can help me. "Yeah." I shove my key in his shriveled yellow face. "I wanna get something out of my fucking box. Let's make that happen, shall we?"

He asks to see the key and I hand it over. It takes him a good thirty seconds to be convinced that it's genuine. His security experts probably taught him exactly how to spot a fake or something because he frantically rubs the engraving of their logo like it's a dormant genie bottle.

"Come with me," he sighs, finally accepting the key's legitimacy.

We walk back to his office and he asks me for two forms of government-issued photo identification. I hand him my passport and driver's license and his eyes move back and forth between the two credentials like he's trying to spot the differences in two not-quite-identical pictures in some magazine for retarded kids.

He pounds on his computer's ergonomically-friendly keyboard with his tiny fingers for a few seconds and brings up my file. "I'm afraid that yours is not the primary name listed under this particular box, Mister Bishop," he reports.

I know that. "I know that. Unfortunately my wife's dead though so she isn't able to vouch for me." I pull her badly-creased death certificate out of my back pocket. The narrator says the bank manager is wholly taken aback by my cavalier attitude regarding the matter which I guess makes sense.

"I'm sorry for your loss," he says. I just nod and affect an air of light solemnity. Might as well patronize the guy I guess. Then the little bastard tells me that the terms of our rental agreement stipulate that in the event of Deborah's death somebody else takes possession of the box besides me.

I'm drawing a complete blank trying to remember the circumstances surrounding our decision to stash my ill-gotten nest egg in a safety deposit box. Nothing's coming back. Nothing. I probably wasn't even there when Debbie signed the papers and shit. "Well who the hell is it then?" I ask, angrily.

The prick clears his throat and tells me that my daughter, Iris, is the only person legally permitted access to the contents of safety deposit box 1138. Fuck. I go on an obscenity-laced tirade and after a few minutes security escorts me out of the building.

«««—»»»

Holbrook's goons are gone by the time I get tossed out of the bank. I know that it's risky returning to my apartment but that's where I've got my stupid daughter's contact info written down so I've got no choice but to go back there.

I run into my landlord on the way into my building and she mumbles something about my overdue rent. The narrator says I call her something awful just to shut her up but I'm pretty sure that's not true.

It takes me a while to find Iris' number and address and right after I finish storing the info in my zPhone the thing starts to vibrate with a blocked number trying to reach me. I answer and it's Roger.

"What's up man?" I hear myself ask.

"Listen. I just got a call from an old acquaintance of ours that owes me a favor." Roger's voice is 'swelling with urgency.' I don't respond and then he says that the Phoenix cops are on their way to my place to arrest me for an out-of-state murder. He asks me where I am and when I tell him he laughs nervously and wishes me luck.

My heart's hammering as I put away my phone and decide to grab my spare pistol since my trusty Beretta's all the way down in my glove compartment and I might run into some shit before I get back to my car. I sprint into my bedroom and pull out the cheap fireproof safe Deborah made me buy when we found out she was pregnant. I fumble with the broken lock for a moment before opening the lid. An invisible wrecking ball slams into my stomach as I look down into an empty case.

I'm pretty sure I could make a solid guess at what caliber of bullet was pulled out of Elliot Zimmerman's skull during his autopsy. Desert Eagle .50. Fuck.

«««—»»»

Phoenix cops are dumb so it doesn't take much effort for me to elude them. They sent three squad cars to my apartment which I guess is about right. I'm racking my brain trying to figure out when someone could've broken into my apartment and stolen my Desert Eagle as I drive away and then I glimpse in my rear view mirror and see a black mini-van bearing down upon me.

«««—»»»

Holbrook's goons try to run me off the road. They ram my rear bumper then pull into my right blind spot, apparently getting ready to implement what's known as the Precision Immobilization Technique. I guess they must've skipped the part of my bio that lists my extensive training in tactical driving because a basic shuffle steering maneuver throws them off and they almost lose control of their vehicle. I shift up a gear and speed through traffic with my right foot pressed as far down as I can force it.

Rush hour's an hour or so away so there aren't too many cars for me to avoid as I negotiate traffic at an extremely high speed, the hemi-powered engine housed within my muscle car outdueling Holbrook's goons' minivan with relative ease. Then the narrator says they hit a nitrous oxide booster and all of a sudden they're right back on my ass.

I spot a vacant dirt lot ahead and recklessly pull into it, my tires spinning wildly as the minivan follows me into a frantic spinout. Our chase seems to go into slow motion as a tornadic cloud of rock and mineral particles envelops us and after a few seconds we're both driving blind. I reach into my glove box to get my trusty Beretta but it's missing now too. Shit.

I take a big risk and drive back out to what I think is the road and luckily there's no one coming when my GTO leaps back onto a stretch of smooth asphalt. Either my pursuers aren't as brave as me or they don't realize I've exited our manmade sand storm because I'm able to escape onto a busy intersection that leads to the highway without spotting the mini-van in any of my mirrors. I exhale a lungful of stale carbon dioxide and then I'm suddenly choking on an acidic juice being served up by my innards. I spit a thick globule of what tastes like bile onto my passenger seat but when I look down at what comes out it looks a lot like blood.

«««—»»»

THE SPARTAK TRIGGER

Leslie's motel obviously isn't safe to visit so I decide I should hide out at one of Roger's safe houses after driving around the valley for a few hours. I call him up and he tells me he'll text me the address and the security code for a nice quiet spot he's got out in Peoria. It takes him a while to send me the info for some reason.

I've got a terrible feeling when I enter the code at the suburban community's gated entrance, like there's going to be a massive explosion as soon as I hit the ENTER button. I breathe a massive sigh of relief when the metallic gate swings open without incident and I drive carefully onto a darkened cul-de-sac 'brimming with eeriness.'

Every bungalow looks the exact same and none of the street lights are on so it takes me a while to find the house Roger apparently leaves unlocked at all times. As soon as I walk through the front door I hit the light switch. I'm not really surprised that the electricity doesn't seem to work.

Right when I finish futilely fighting with the dormant power system my smartphone starts to vibrate again and it's a blocked ID so I assume that it's Roger calling. "Hello?" No one responds. "Who is this?" I demand, allegedly 'awash in frantic desperation.'

There's a long pause and I'm about ready to hang up when an excited female voice nearly bursts through the line: "Good evening Mister Bishop, my name is Kelly and I'm pleased to inform you that you've been specially selected to become a member of the Super Budget Discount Rewards Club! For quality control purposes our conversation will be recorded from here on in. If you indeed elect to subscribe to this amazing club today I've been authorized by my manager to pass along a complimentary set of vouchers valued at over two hundred dollars for use at any pre-authorized retailer throughout the continental United States. We have your credit card ending with the digits five-three-oh-nine on file so if you simply state the authorization term 'okay' we can go ahead and sign you up to be a Super Budget Discount Rewards Club Member at our introductory rate of five dollars per month, a fee which will increase by increments of two dollars every other week for the duration of the contract, which will of course be two calendar years beginning with your first billing cycle. I will remind you that by joining our club today, and today only, you will receive a retail voucher package valued at over two hundred dollars which may be used on any items you desire. If you would like to proceed, simply state the word 'okay' okay, Mister Bishop?"

I start breathing heavily and ask Kelly what she's wearing.

"I'm sorry, Mister Bishop but we aren't allowed to give out personal information to clients." The young-sounding slut's still perky as fuck. "So if you just want to go ahead and say the word 'okay' we'll get you registered in the Super Budget Discount Rewards Club and have those vouchers mailed to your current address as soon as possible, does that sound good?"

"I want to cut your thigh open with a rusty knife and stick my hard, AIDS-infected dick inside the open wound."

"That doesn't sound pleasant at all Mister Bishop but I will let you know that SlashCo Incorporated is one of the retailers authorized to accept Super Discount Budget Saver vouchers so you would in fact be able to purchase a new, rust-free knife with the introductory membership package we'll be sending your way as soon as you issue a verbal contract, which as I stated earlier can simply be achieved by repeating the word 'okay' okay?"

A silicon switch goes off in my brain and I tell Kelly all of the terrible things I want to do to her, really messed up stuff involving still-born babies and hot curling irons and such. The narrator relays the tirade verbatim but then the editor steps in and vehemently objects to the whole exchange so my voice stops emitting sound and the phone line just goes dead.

I spend a sleepless night sprawled out atop an ultra-thin carpet, my mind racing wildly to try and make sense of everything that's happened in the last forty-eight hours. It's been pretty insane, huh?

THE SPARTAK TRIGGER

«‹‹—›››

Roger's standing over me talking but his words are buried beneath what sounds like electric guitar feedback. My ears eventually make out what he's saying and he ends a lengthy spiel with: "You look like shit."

He has to gather every once of strength he can muster in helping me get to my feet and when I'm finally vertical he slugs me in the shoulder and tells me that I've got to get it together. "Yeah," I say. "That's on my list of things to do."

"What the hell have you got yourself into?" Roger's surveying me with extreme concern. Fair enough.

"That's the thing, Rog." My voice is impossibly faint. "I've got no fucking clue."

We walk out onto a brick patio and he retrieves a pair of lawn chairs from behind a decrepit shed on the far side of the felt lawn. I sit down and everything is spinning out of control, like I just got off of some vomit-inducing ride at a carny-infested fairground. Roger puts his hand on my shoulder and offers me a drink from his hip flask and I take a stiff swig which sobers me right up.

"Do you at least know what murder they're after you for?" Roger asks after we spend a moment staring 'docilely' into a brilliantly blue sky.

"Some asshole in San Diego I never even killed."

"Shitty."

"Yeah."

"So why do they think you did it?"

I tell my former partner all about Sancus, Tetrace, ChumSpot, my missing/awkwardly-introduced guns (which the narrator now claims once belonged to the Russian guy from *Star Trek*), Dave, Holbrook, Leslie. Everything. Roger repeatedly interrupts to tell me that none of what I'm saying makes sense, that it's too fantastic to be true. I don't disagree but when he catches me fighting back a tear he believes every word I've said. He knows I'm not that good of an actor.

Roger asks me what my plan is and I tell him: "I've gotta get my daughter to go get my cash out and then I'm gonna disappear down to Mexico."

"Well I doubt you'll make it across the border using your own passport, being wanted for murder and all," he says, almost as an afterthought. This hadn't occurred to me for some reason and my head tilts downwards in shame as I realize how stupid I sounded just now.

"I can't help you with your daughter." Roger stands up and stretches his arms out. "But I can definitely help get you across the border." The narrator sounds exceptionally pompous as he leads an ultra-quick survey course covering Roger's meteoric rise through the Arizona underworld. He tells us that the bastard had made enough contacts through our kickback scams to start his career off in a position akin to upper management right after the force granted us early retirement in lieu of an embarrassing show trial and then went on to traffic drugs, guns, yadda yadda blah blah blah. Some of what he says is news to me though—especially the part about the profitable indentured servant enterprise Roger's recently launched as part of his extensive human smuggling operation.

We walk back out front and open the garage to stash my car away and there's a huge rattlesnake hissing at us as soon as the unpainted wooden door swings upwards. I scream like a tweenaged girl when the thing hisses at us but Roger just laughs and shoots it to pieces with an Uzi he pulls out of a cool-looking holster housed inside the brown leather jacket he's rocking.

"Aren't you worried about your neighbors?" I ask after the blaring gunfire ceases. Roger shakes his head and explains to me that the entire community is comprised of abandoned homes that the banks took possession of following the big mortgage crisis a few years back.

"The only people living in this neighborhood are illegals from down south that wouldn't say boo if you pissed on their leg."

The narrator goes into an impassioned diatribe about how impoverished minority immigrants squatting in the former homes of foolhardy white people who bought houses they couldn't afford effectively serves as a brilliant allegory for the volatile continuum of the American Dream. I'm momentarily distracted by the oddly-compelling rant and barely notice as Roger grabs my zPhone out of my hand and throws it in the air, blasting it apart with his gun like he's a fake cowboy performing at some tourist trap over in Tombstone.

"What'd you do that for?!"

"They can track you anywhere in the world with that thing."

"Really?"

"Yeah, really."

"But I had my daughter's address and phone number stored in there!" I fling my arms in the air in protest.

"So we'll just look her up in the phone book or Tetrace her or something, what's wrong with you?"

Shame pulsates through me once again and I try to think of something witty to say but then we both hear a thunderous tire squeal and turn to face a speeding black mini-van headed in our direction. Without saying a word Roger opens fire on Holbrook's goons with his Uzi. After its windshield's shattered at the behest of a barrage of bullets the minivan crashes headfirst into a lamp-post. The scar-chinned prick who'd mocked my football career stumbles out of the passenger seat covered in blood and broken glass. He unleashes a bellowing death cry and pulls out his CZ-75. He gets off a couple of wild shots that miss us badly while my cowboy bodyguard retrieves a fresh cartridge from his jacket.

Roger finishes the wounded shithead off with a dozen bullets to the face. We inspect the smoldering minivan to make sure the driver is also dead. He is. He most definitely is.

We hop into Roger's SUV and burn rubber back down the cul-de-sac. The incredibly loud jazz fusion blaring from a pair of customized Japanese speakers makes an oddly appropriate soundtrack to our retreat from the grisly scene.

⟪⟪⟪—⟫⟫⟫

A ninety-minute car ride is spent in abject silence as Roger takes me up to his super-secret hideout up in Prescott Valley. Not even Roger's top lieutenants know about this place apparently, so he says at least.

Once we get to his remote cabin Roger wishes me luck with my daughter and tells me he's got to get back to the city. He tells me there's plenty of food in the fridge here and writes down the number for the secure landline at the place I'll be staying at for the time being. This makes me think about my zPhone for the first time since it was blown to smithereens and the narrator takes this as a cue to launch into another harangue. He declares that a 'peculiar, grief-like sensation is welling within the very depths of my soul' and that it feels like a part of me has been amputated or something, like I'm an old war veteran scratching at a phantom limb now that I don't have my smartphone. I think this is meant to be a lot more poignant than it sounds but since none of it has any bearing on anything I just let him blather on and on.

Roger watches me get out of his SUV, grab my bag, and meander up to the cabin's solid oak-wrapped entrance. "I'll call you tomorrow!" he shouts as he drives away. Part of me wishes he'd just back up and run me over, put me out of my misery. No such luck.

⟪⟪⟪—⟫⟫⟫

Roger's northern hideaway has a lot more amenities that the bungalow back in Peoria. The lights work and there's even a flat-screen television in the living room. Digital cable. Nice. High-speed internet. Beauty.

I turn on the local news and pass out on this tacky finished-walnut futon while I'm watching some mustachioed meteorologist talk about how hot it's going to be this week. Tell me something I don't know.

THE SPARTAK TRIGGER

«‹‹—›»›

Iris doesn't seem to recognize my voice at all and when I tell her it's her father calling a 'palpable tension' inundates the line.

"What the hell do you want?" she yelps. "Some cops were over here the other day y'know. They was asking if I'd seen you lately."

"What'd you tell them?"

"That we haven't spoken since mom's funeral. That you're a fucking prick and I hope they catch you for whatever the hell you've gone and done now."

I tell her to calm down and ask her if anyone else has been to see her. "Yeah." She takes a deep breath and starts to chill somewhat. "Some old creepy guy who looks like he spends a lot of time in a tanning bed was over here asking about you." Holbrook. Fuck.

It doesn't matter that he went to see her I guess since she didn't have any worthwhile information to give him regarding my whereabouts and whatnot. I try to tell her I'm sorry that we haven't seen each other much lately but she's not buying it and tells me to fuck off before slamming the phone down.

I have to call back eight times before she picks up again and then I quickly promise her ten grand in cash before she has the chance to hang up. "I'm listening." Her timbre is swimming through a strange mixture of contempt and enthusiasm.

"Thought that might get your attention." The narrator briefly summarizes the tumultuous relationship my daughter and I have had, mentioning stuff like when she ran away from home at fifteen and the time I slugged her for stealing an eight ball from my stash. Whatever. That's all in the past. Fuck it. Fuck it all.

Iris agrees to meet me in Glendale and retrieve my cash from the bank in exchange for a generous cut of the loot. She asks me when she should be there and I remember that I don't have a car so I tell her I'll call her back after I talk to her uncle Roger.

"For fuck's sake, you're still hanging around with that retarded piece of shit drunkard?"

"Watch your language, young lady!" A few seconds after this leaves my mouth we both start laugh hysterically as if we're sharing an elaborate inside joke which I guess is true in a backwards, perverse kind of way.

‹‹‹—›››

Roger pulls into the driveway at four in the morning and bursts through the front door with a half-naked skank hanging off of each arm. "Wake the hell up, partner!" he yells, not seeing that I'm wide-awake and watching an old World War II movie on his flat-screen.

"Where the hell have you been?" I float up off the couch like our planet's gravity's been suspended for a split second and then I'm standing over by the island kitchenette thingy. "I've been cooped up in this place for a week now!"

"Do you wanna get your fuck on or not, Shaner?" Roger's words are spilling over one another and he's staggering badly. I fleetingly hope he's only been drinking but the two broads he's got with him look like goddamned crack whores so I'd bet the house on him being high as a kite as well.

When we wake up the next day both of the girls have vanished, as has Roger's wallet, his watch, and his Italian-made loafers. He tells me in his best prohibition-era gangster voice that he's going to have some local bikers find the bitches and beat them both to within an inch of their lives. Whatever.

‹‹‹—›››

During our drive back down to Phoenix Roger tells me that his source at the police department recently informed him that I'm the sole suspect in the Zimmerman murder at present. I ask him why they haven't released any information about me to the press yet and he's not sure. "They're probably embarrassed I guess, seein' as how you're an ex-cop and all."

THE SPARTAK TRIGGER

"Yeah, I guess we're not exactly Hall of Fame alumni, huh?" The fake beard Roger bought for me itches like you wouldn't believe and the bad toupee he probably found in a gutter somewhere looks utterly ridiculous. I tell him the disguise is stupid but he tells me it'll do for the time being. It's just temporary. I use Roger's cell phone to call Iris and tell her to meet me at this dirty Tex-Mex restaurant called Taco Grande in Glendale in an hour.

«««—»»»

My daughter's waiting for me at a corner booth and she doesn't stand up to greet me. Her face is a 'mask of sternness.' I sit down and she snickers at the sight of my shitty disguise.

"You look like an idiot," she says flatly.

"That's the idea." I switch the salt and peppershakers' positions atop the table for some reason. "The cops are looking for a ruggedly handsome, dashing playboy-type. They'll never spot me looking like this."

Iris tries not to laugh but can't help herself. She looks so much like her mother it's scary. I'm forced to be reminded of this as the narrator goes and describes her appearance to us. Wavy chestnut hair. Delicate facial features. Low-hanging ear lobes. Pencil-thin eyebrows. Like I said—scary. There's a volatile ignorance behind her eyes that Deborah didn't have though. The white trash DNA my parents had in great supply is deeply-entrenched within her, always has been. Too bad. She could've been something if her maternal genetics had won out.

Our waitress comes and takes our drink order—cerveza for me and an unsweetened ice tea for Iris.

"Come on, I'm buying," I tell Iris after our waitress walks away. "You can order whatever you want."

"I'm not drinking these days." She struggles to stand and adopts a lurching pose that shows off the substantial bump protruding from her midsection.

"Wow." That's all I can say for however long it takes for the room to stop spinning. "How far along are you?"

"Five months." Iris sits back down.

"Who's the father?"

"Not too sure to be honest."

"Well I'm certainly glad your mother isn't alive to hear you say that. Do you know the gender yet?"

"Yup." Her tone is almost wistful. "I'm gonna have me a boy."

Iris knows full well that I always wanted a son and she looks at me with remorse-filled eyes as I digest the information she's just fed me. I'm going to be a grandfather. The narrator goes off on a tangent about how I'd tried to raise Iris like a boy for a while, making her play baseball and shit when she was in grade school. This was after Deborah learned she couldn't have another kid, which was right around the time I started using pretty heavily. Then the narrator announces to everyone that I'm undergoing some kind of 'dramatic catharsis' and that my entire plan to escape to Mexico is now going to be abandoned so I can try and be a part of my grandson's life somehow. Another lucky guess.

Our waitress brings us our drinks and I'm too choked up to speak. Iris asks me what's wrong and I excuse myself. The men's room is a cauldron of anxiety and I grasp the sides of a filthy sink firmly with both hands as I stare vacantly into a grime-ridden mirror. My nose starts to bleed pretty badly and I think I might pass out but then I don't.

«««—»»»

Iris doesn't have any problems getting into the vault apparently and when I ask her about the little Asian guy she giggles and mentions that he kept sneezing in a hilariously meek manner the entire time she was in there. She opens her handbag and sixty grand in illegally-attained hard currency tastes fresh air for the first time in nearly two decades.

"Where do you wanna do divvy up the loot?" Iris asks, coyly.

THE SPARTAK TRIGGER

"Don't worry about it, kiddo." I put my right hand on her pregnant stomach and she doesn't look happy about it but doesn't tell me to stop. "You keep the whole thing. Keep it all."

"What about Mexico?" My untrusting daughter shoots me an 'acrimonious glare.' "What about the warrant they've got out for you?"

"Never was much a fan of tequila to be honest. More of a whiskey man myself." I let go of her swollen belly. "I think I'll stick around here, see how things play out. Maybe even play catch with my grandson in a few years."

"If you think I'd take my boy to visit you in some god awful prison you've got another thing coming."

I grab Iris by the shoulders and give her an embrace that she only briefly tries to resist. She starts to weep as soon as her head's pressed against my chest and I tell her that everything's going to be okay.

"I didn't kill that guy in San Diego," I say. "I swear on your mother's grave that I didn't."

"So what are you going to do?" she blurts out between sobs.

"I'm not sure, kiddo. I guess I'll figure something out."

We stand like this in the Taco Grande parking lot for a long while, neither one of us wanting the moment to end.

«««—»»»

Roger tells me I'm crazy when I tell him I want to stay in the U.S. and try to clear my name somehow. "You've got the cops after you, some government spook sent a pair of thugs out to take you down and your boss was killed at the exact same time you were framed for a high-profile murder." Roger's shouting at me as if I'm deaf and dumb. "And, on top of all of that, you just gave away your entire life savings to your daughter just because she's pregnant with a kid that might be half-black or something. You're out of your fucking mind, Bish—you're screwed if you stick around here, screwed!"

I pretend to take a moment to consider everything Roger's said, just to be polite. "Look, I'm innocent. Somebody set me up.

They did a good fucking job of it too. The real killer's out there and I've got a good idea who hired him."

"Who?"

"Tetrace."

"The online search engine? 'Don't chase it—Tetrace it?' You think a goddamn website set you up? That's it—we're taking you over to the loony bin right now." He grabs me by both shoulders with his hove-like hands and pulls me towards the front door of his condo. "It's for the best, don't fight it." I manage to break free, not entirely sure if he's kidding or not.

"No, listen," I protest. "I told you before—their head office had us on a retainer. They had us probe at least a half dozen of their execs in the last few months, mostly loyalty tests."

Roger looks at me 'perplexedly' and I get ready to explain to him what I mean but he refrains from asking. His wiry frame is hunched over slightly, his wrinkle-framed eyes bloodshot. I can only guess at what the hell else he's dealing with at the moment. Roger's expression melts into a rueful smile right before he sighs and tells me he'll do anything he can to help me out.

"You're gonna need a whole new identity, partner," he says, shaking his head in disbelief. "Only way you'll be able to get around. You were right by the way, that fake beard does make you look retarded."

"You must have some people that can arrange a new identity for me—big shot criminal kingpin like yourself?"

Roger unleashes what the narrator labels a 'roguish guffaw' that lasts a disconcertingly long while and eventually makes me start to shudder. "You know what," he says. "I actually know someone who can totally help you out. He's bat shit crazy too, you guys'll get along great."

"Who is he?" I ask.

"We just call him 'The Wizard.'"

"'The Wizard?'" he's not going to turn me into a newt or something is he?"

"No but that's about all this guy *can't* do. He got the nickname after he won a big video game tournament when he was a little kid, out in California. Now he's a damned good digital security troubleshooter slash hacker. Solely responsible for making Arizona the most dangerous state for identity theft in the country. This guy can make anyone into somebody else—even Mexicans."

"Sounds good. Let's pay him a visit."

I follow Roger out to his SUV. We tell each other dirty jokes we've each heard a million times before during the drive out to Chandler.

《《—》》

It turns out The Wizard lives in a small trailer on a massive dirt lot near the Gilbert border. He doesn't appear to have any neighbors for miles on end.

The trailer itself looks like it should be condemned. Its exterior is caked in filth and the walls are crooked, as if designed by an LSD-addicted architect. We approach the front door, slowly.

"I haven't been out to this place in a while," Roger warns me. "Not sure what he'll have going on in here."

"How do you know he's even home?" I ask. "You never called or texted him or anything."

"Don't worry. He never leaves. I guess he's got some condition, 'agrachiaphobia' or something like that. Makes him deathly afraid of the outdoors and shit"

"Great."

Roger knocks on the door and what sounds like an old school sci-fi robot immediately demands to know who it is out of a tiny speaker situated above the door frame. "Mr. Wizard!" Roger yells up into the sky. "It's your employer. Open up."

"Very well," the mechanical voice drones.

A hydraulic hissing sound begins to emit from behind the decrepit-looking wooden door just as plumes of steam secrete out of the concrete slab we're standing on. I ask Roger what the hell's going on and he just laughs playfully as we begin to descend into the ground.

Within a manner of seconds we're staring into a gigantic bunker filled with a cornucopia of technological gadgetry and the narrator's trying to tell me that I should've said 'matter of seconds.' Either way, dozens of computer monitors are situated at haphazardly-stationed terminals throughout a sterile, metallic-walled chamber littered with circuit boards, loose wires, and empty pizza boxes and I'm trying to figure out how the hell anyone could live in a place like this. At the far end of the room a daunting, high-backed office chair is facing a colossal video screen that looks as if its been stolen from the secret lair of a billionaire playboy who moonlights as a masked vigilante.

"Mr. Gormley. It's been a while. Quite a while indeed." The nasal, monotone voice addressing us sounds as if it's reciting a dreary courtroom transcript.

"Yeah, sorry Wiz, been real busy lately. You know how it is." Roger's fidgeting slightly and I try and remember the last time I'd seen him act even remotely nervous. *When Internal Affairs first came down on us maybe?*

"Who's your friend?" the voice asks.

"Wiz, this is Shane Bishop—an old buddy of mine. He needs help."

"And exactly what kind of help does Shane Bishop need?"

"The kind only you can provide. The kind you'll get double your normal rate for fulfilling."

The giant chair slowly rotates towards us and all-of-a-sudden the mutated, acne-scarred face of The Wizard is all I can see. A look of intense curiosity is beaming through his narrow, black eyes. "Well then, it's a pleasure to meet you, Shane Bishop."

I glance over at Roger who nods absently. "Yeah," I say. "Likewise."

The Wizard recognizes me from a police network he's hacked into and giddily asks me if I'm guilty of the crime of which I'm accused. I tell him no and he's apparently heartbroken.

THE SPARTAK TRIGGER

"That's too bad," he laments. "It would indeed be an honor to meet the man that blew away that scumbag Elliot Zimmerman. Did you know that he stole the idea for ChumSpot from me?"

I shake my head. "No. I did not know that."

The narrator seems to be unsure as to how accurate The Wizard's claim is. He does acknowledge that he was a classmate of Zimmerman's at some fancy boarding school out east a few years back.

"Sorry to disappoint you...Wiz." I feel weird calling the guy that but I guess he must like it or else he would've put a stop to it at some point, right?

"Anyhow," Roger interjects. "I've gotta be getting back to the city." He turns to face me and punches me in the arm with a surprising amount of force, making me wonder if it was meant as a fraternal gesture or maybe something else altogether. "I'll be back tomorrow to check in on you two characters."

"Always a pleasure, Roger," The Wizard exclaims. I can't tell if he's being sarcastic or not. "Can I assume you'll be bringing me my latest commission check with you upon your aforementioned return to my abode?" Roger apologizes for forgetting but the narrator says he's got the money in his car. He's not sure why Roger doesn't want to hand it over to The Wizard at the moment. Whatever. None of our business I guess.

"Good luck, partner." Roger winks at me as he steps back onto the hydraulic platform and is swiftly transported back up to the surface.

The Wizard invites me over to his terminal. He presses a button and the pile of junk on his floor just disappears so I guess I must've been a hologram or something even though that doesn't make a goddamn lick of sense. The Wizard presses another button and a small metallic stool emerges near his massive chair. I sit down and notice that my host's got a big shit-eating grin on his face.

"So, Roger tells me you're the best at this stuff." A feeling of extreme unease overtakes me as I try to establish eye contact with one of the ugliest human beings I've ever encountered. I make a couple of awkward, asinine comments about how I read somewhere that the authorities have been cracking down on digital crime lately and then there's a painful silence that only seems to bother one of us in the room.

"Yes, well, luckily for me the government exclusively employs community college dropouts in their digital crime units," The Wizard says eventually. "Those morons couldn't hack their way out of a paper bag. No way in hell they'll ever… CAPTCHA…me!"

I stare blankly at The Wizard as the narrator groans and reluctantly expounds the terrible pun that was just made. I groan as well after I understand it. *Awful, just awful.*

"So. Shane." Undeterred by his poorly-received witticism, The Wizard takes a bite out of a large strand of licorice that's appeared out of thin air. "Why don't you tell me how exactly how you've managed to find yourself in this cumbersome predicament you're in?"

«««—»»»

It takes longer than I'd anticipated for me to tell The Wizard my story. This is mainly because he keeps interrupting me to randomly talk about various conspiracy theories he's been researching in his spare time. His social skills are beyond abysmal, his countenance that of a heavily-caffeinated toddler.

Over the course of our multi-hour discussion The Wizard somehow manages to explain to me how the 9/11 attacks had actually been orchestrated by a conglomerate of private American flag manufacturers, the steroid scandals in baseball were cooked up by the government in order to cover up an even more sinister plot involving the splicing of alien and human DNA, and how Mormon extremists were responsible for that big oil spill in the Gulf of Mexico a few years back. I manage to get in a few words here and there.

THE SPARTAK TRIGGER

Once I finally get to the part of MY story where Roger threatens to institutionalize me I ask The Wizard if he's been paying attention. I'm shocked when he then quickly surmises everything I've said in a single sentence: "Okay, so you're a professional frame-up expert who's somewhat-ironically been framed for a high-profile murder himself and now you need me to set you up with a new identity so you can make use of your finely-hones detective skills and go about clearing your name so you'll get to spend time with your grandson once he's born. That about right?"

"Uh. Yeah."

"Okay then." The Wizard turns to face his NASA-like computer screen and begins to type. His thin fingers are immediately a blur of motion atop a boomerang-shaped keyboard.

"What makes this whole thing interesting is the involvement of Tetrace." The Wizard's eyes bulge out of his head as he speaks, his gaze intently fixated upon a fast-moving stream of bright green computer language.

"Why is that exactly?" I ask.

The Wizard, somewhat extraneously, explains to us that Tetrace has conquered every facet of the internet-based product and service industries since emerging victorious from what he refers to as the 'search engine wars' ten years ago. I try to tell him that I already know all of this and that it really doesn't matter but he doesn't let me interrupt him.

"Tetrace pretty much controls everything you see on the mainstream internet," he says, quite likely editorializing and/or outright lying. "They filter and censor all of the stories that run on tNews, sometimes changing certain details without explanation. They have access to everyone with a tMail account's personal correspondences. They secretly run every successful SPAM mail system, making millions from idiots buying discount erectile dysfunction pills and shit. The government pays them to alert them of anyone using their site to search for 'how to make homemade bombs' or 'how to dispose of a dead body' and whatnot that but I've heard they sometimes blackmail certain individuals in exchange for keeping their illicit searches from the authorities…"

The Wizard gasps as if emerging from a swimming pool at the end of a high-stakes breath-holding contest. "They have their own administrators running infopedia, which kids have grown up accepting as absolute fact." The Wizard's tone is becoming increasingly histrionic as he continues to ramble on. "WatchThis—the most powerful new media outlet on the planet—is theirs as well. Some people, myself included, believe that Tetra-Earth is in fact the first step towards having everyone on the planet under video surveillance at all times. They even clandestinely run all of the most popular porn sites and gambling portals. ChumSpot was the last web phenomenon that they didn't control completely, and now they've managed to gain control of that as well."

I mention how they'd used Sancus quite a bit in the past six months—mostly for loyalty tests—and that I think it was them who probably set me up. The Wizard stops typing and turns to face me.

"So." He begins stroking his sullen chin like an intrigued professor. "They've been trying to weed out disloyal employees—get rid of anyone they can't trust completely. Then they purchase the internet's top social media site and frame you for the murder of its top executive." I can tell the wheels of motion are moving along at immeasurable speeds within the confines of his brilliant, warped mind.

"While all this is going on," The Wizard continues, "a special congressional subcommittee is created to investigate Tetrace's potentially-unconstitutional monopoly, which is inherently difficult given the splintered nature of their business model not to mention the countless phantom slash secret partnership agreements they've developed in the last decade. Plus the web's legal boundaries have yet to be outlined definitively, making the whole investigation largely theoretical, abstract even."

THE SPARTAK TRIGGER

I hadn't heard that Tetrace was being investigated by the government but I pretend to know all about it as The Wizard turns his attention back to the computer station that now seems as if it's an extension of his anemic body.

"Now, the most vocal opponents of the Tetrace monopoly are Senator Vance Turner from Georgia and Senator Michael Fulton from Ohio. Both of these cats are up for re-election this month, and both are expected to win their seats back with tremendous ease. Moderate right wingers, clean-cut All-American-types, you know the score."

The Wizard offers me a bottle of some energy drink I've never heard of and I politely decline. He continues to think out loud in a rapid-fire, stream-of-consciousness manner. He eventually postulates that Tetrace is planning on rigging these two key senatorial elections using ChumSpot somehow. He speculates that Zimmerman must've somehow gotten wind of the scheme after they'd made their deal and they had to have him bumped off. *Makes sense I guess… Well, maybe not. Oh well.*

"What about Daniels? And the broad up in Seattle?" I ask, boisterously. "And Holbrook—how does he fit into this whole thing?"

"Well, that's what you're going to find out when you infiltrate the company and help me hack into their mainframe." The pseudo-smirk The Wizard is flashing is unlike anything I've ever seen, as if he's using a facial expression from another planet—which could very well be the case. "There will definitely be a digital trail of some kind that they've left behind—emails, files—but their firewall is impenetrable to an external attack," he explains. "I can only gain access through a remote server that needs to be installed manually, up-close-and-personal that is."

"What the hell are you talking about?" My own voice sounds unfamiliar, usurped by a raspy, dissonant timbre. The narrator's moaning about being forced to make such a massive information dump in such a short time and in such a jumbled and intentionally-confusing manner. Whatever. Meanwhile, the room's spinning slowly, gratingly—like a rusty carousel.

The Wizard tells me that there's a job opening for a graveyard shift janitor at Tetrace's San Jose office. "Bernie Roberts just applied for the position and his résumé is immaculate."

"Who's Bernie Roberts?" The room stops rotating just as abruptly as it started.

"You are." The Wizard points at his glowing computer screen and the digital images of a dozen pieces of identification for Bernard Anthony Roberts—passport, driver's license, credit cards—are overlapping each other in a neatly-organized circular pattern. The photo brandished upon each piece of ID looks like a fat, densely-bearded, horn-rimmed-glasses-wearing, shorn-skulled version of me.

"Wow." I'm genuinely impressed, which is rare. "Roger told me you were good but… Wow."

"Let's get started!" The Wizard gallantly exclaims. "This is going to be great—we'll clear your name, solve a murder case, and take down the most powerful new media conglomerate in the world all at the same time. It'll make one hell of an entry on my next blog!"

The narrator is exceedingly skeptical about the whole thing but I don't really care. He can go straight to hell as far as I'm concerned.

I'm sweating my balls off in the back row of a near-empty bus. The latex fat suit The Wizard provided me with doesn't offer much in the way of ventilation. We make a transfer in Los Angeles and I spend the thirty-minute layover sitting in an air-conditioned bathroom after poking a few holes in the uncomfortable getup with a pen. "You'll get used to it" he'd told me while he was digging the thing out of a cluttered closet in the deepest part of his bunker. Idiot.

I get back on the bus and I'm about ready to die of boredom after a few hours when I spot a tattered paperback novel sitting in an unoccupied seat. I get up and grab the book, which is called *Triple Bluff*. I guess it's a pretty good title.

THE SPARTAK TRIGGER

The main guy in the novel is a degenerate gigolo who ends up going on a date with some super rich widow and then they get married soon afterwards. The whole time this guy is planning on killing the woman to inherit all of her money but then it turns out that she's not rich after all and has a big insurance policy out on her new, young husband. By the time he realizes this she's already poisoned him and he dies a painful, spastic death in the billiards room of their mansion as the woman watches and callously laughs at him. She ends up getting away with the whole thing scot-free so good for her I guess.

«««—»»»

I check into this disgusting motel out in the middle of nowhere and get out of my disguise as soon as I'm alone in my room. The fake credit cards The Wizard gave me all seem to work fine. He told me that Bernie's digitally-manufactured credit rating isn't very good, which means that the credit card companies love him and will keep raising his spending limit until he's completely fucked. Good stuff.

I jump into bed and turn on the TV and some hyperactive bald dude with a lazy eye who sounds like he's from Boston is telling me to send me in all of the gold I've got laying around my house in exchange for cash. Then the same guy's appearing in the next commercial but his accent's slightly different—Alaskan maybe—and now he's demanding that I gather up all of my unused electronic devices and mail them to him as well, also in exchange for cash. Weirdness.

«««—»»»

I can't sleep so I go for a walk and spot one of those gaudy multiplex movie theaters at the end of the block called The Crystal Palace and I find myself being pulled towards it as if I'm caught in a tractor beam or something. The marquee is advertising that they're showing all three of the 'Live Snuff' films back-to-back-to-back beginning tonight at midnight. I look at my watch and its 11:57pm so I go buy a ticket from a pimply-faced teenager who tries to make small talk about the weather but I just ignore him.

There's no one in line at the canteen and I treat myself to a gluttonous array of junk food—candy, soda, popcorn with extra butter, ice cream. Fuck it, who cares?

The first installment in the 'Live Snuff' trilogy has already started playing by the time I find a seat near the back of the theater. A couple of college kids are making out in the row right in front of me and I watch them for a bit and by the time I realize that it's in fact two dudes going at it one of the characters in the movie is being killed with a power tool by who I assume is probably supposed to be the main villain. I'm surprised at how authentic the sound effects are and then when the stage floor starts to fill with blood I realize that what I'm watching isn't a movie—it's a play.

«««—»»»

The human resources assistant at Tetrace's smallest branch is telling me all about some bullshit employee benefits program they've got. She's not bad looking but way too chipper. It's like she's auditioning for a part in an afterschool special about the dangers of amphetamine abuse.

I keep nodding and telling her that I've got twenty years of experience in the custodial arts. She says my credentials are impressive and that my references all checked out fine and then she takes me down to the basement to meet the head janitor. He just grunts and tells me I'll be working the graveyard shift as soon as the paperwork's all processed so I guess I've got the job.

The HR lady has me sign all kinds of forms and a super-long confidentiality agreement. They make me piss in a cup and I almost spill the clean sample I brought with me when my stupid allergies force a sneeze out of me.

THE SPARTAK TRIGGER

«««—»»»

I call The Wizard on the miniature cell phone he hooked me up with when I get back to my motel and I give him the good news. He's distracted by some blog-related nonsense but congratulates me and quickly reminds me how to install the remote server thingy he gave me once I'm alone in an office at Tetrace. I tell him I understand implicitly and he hangs up after wishing me good luck.

«««—»»»

There's a pretty decent strip club not too far from my motel so I spend a couple of days there charging meals, drinks and lap dances to Bernie's credit cards. On the second night I get a bit excited and grab one of the girls so the bouncers rough me up and toss me out onto the street. Assholes.

«««—»»»

I'm worried that my new boss might shadow me on my first night at Tetrace but when I check in early at half-past-eleven he gives me a quick rundown of the building, shows me where all the cleaning supplies are and then gets the fuck out of dodge. Can't blame him; I'd probably do the same thing If I were him. It's not like they're putting me in charge of a nuclear silo or something.

As far as I can tell I'm the only person in the whole building aside from a security guard who's reading a soft core porno mag down on the ground floor. There's a bunch of cameras all over the place though so I go along with the janitor ruse and do a half-decent job of mopping the top two floors for a couple of hours.

When I make it to the third-highest floor I subtly nudge a security camera out of its shooting lane and jimmy my way into the office of this branch's business development manager. The

Wizard's gadget fits perfectly into the data port of this guy's computer. Some encryption algorithm logs me in and I run back into the hallway to make sure no one's around before I send my accomplice a text message to let him know that I'm plugged into Tetrace's system.

The gizmo I smuggled into the building lights up like a Korochun Tree a few seconds later and I stand back as the computer seems to begin operating itself. I leave the office to let The Wizard do his thing and I spend a half-hour doing some more mopping.

I text The Wizard again to see if he's done and when he doesn't respond I go back up to the office to check on the remote server. When I open the door a rakish figure is standing behind an empty desk, looming ominously like an evil specter in some shadowy vortex. I stand frozen for a few seconds as the translucent silhouette strikes a match and slowly raises it towards a cigarette protruding limply from an odd-shaped head. Once the small flame from the match casts its 'meager glow' upon the figure's face my heart stops beating altogether.

Special Agent Jonathan Holbrook is standing ten feet away from me.

«««—»»»

Holbrook takes several drags from his cigarette before he starts talking. His words blast through the darkness like a pre-dawn air raid: "Good to see you again, Shane."

The narrator uses several fancy-sounding words I don't understand as he describes the scene unfolding, my body and mind suddenly numb to everything around me. Holbrook tosses The Wizard's gadget at me and compliments me on my attempt to hack into Tetrace's mainframe.

"You've proven yourself remarkably resourceful. I was indeed shocked when I'd heard Stuart and Michael had been killed. They were both ex-Marines you know." Holbrook blows a perfectly-symmetrical smoke ring and issues a 'dissembling chuckle.' "I don't mind telling you that it cost us a pretty penny to lure them out of the mercenary game."

I assume he's talking about the two bastards Roger blew away down in Peoria but I don't have a chance to ask him for clarification before I'm distracted by the distinct sound of a revolver cocking behind my head. I close my eyes and wait for a shot but it doesn't come.

"This is my new assistant—Frederick," Holbrook bellows joyously. "Frederick, Shane. Shane, Frederick."

"The pleasure's all yours," a thick Australian accent hisses into my right ear. I swallow a massive lump of stress and tell the thug behind me that I loved him in *Young Einstein*.

"Your friends are quite gifted it would seem," Holbrook says, abruptly extinguishing his cigarette upon the wall nearest him. "This new identity you've been given passed all of our security checks, including one designed by the White House's former digital security chief. Impressive, very impressive indeed."

I tell Holbrook to kiss my ass and his Aussie dog smacks me in the back of the head with the butt end of his gun, knocking me to the ground. He follows up with a few kicks to the midsection but they don't really hurt all that much since I'm still wearing the fat suit required to play the role of Bernie Roberts, custodian.

"Watch your mouth, Tubby," Holbrook's mountainous bodyguard snarls.

"If you're gonna kill me just do it!" I cry out. "I hate long waits."

"Oh, I don't plan on killing you," Holbrook tells me, a dash of 'playful menace' in his voice. "I have a job offer for you."

"I've already a job," I reply.

"No you don't." Holbrook takes a large, purposeful step towards me. "Bernie Roberts does."

"Good point." I spit out some blood. "So what kind of position are you prepared to offer me? I assume that's who you've been working for this whole time then, am I right?"

"Indeed." Holbrook giggles absently for a moment before readopting what the narrator refers to as a 'portentous demeanor.' "What we'd like to offer you is an opportunity to reclaim the pathetic excuse of a life you seem to hold so dear."

Holbrook puts on a pair of black leather gloves and acts like he's performing a fucking magic trick as he reaches into his jacket pocket and pulls out a gun that looks a lot like my missing Desert Eagle. He presents it to me as if he's a salesman at some high-end auction house. "I assume you recognize this weapon?"

I nod and Holbrook motions for his goon to pick me up off the ground, which he does with remarkable ease.

Holbrook puts the gun away and continues. "You're not a complete idiot so I can assume you realize that we handed your Beretta over to the detectives investigating the Zimmerman case down in San Diego. It was, in fact, one of two guns used in the murder, and it, of course, has your fingerprints all over it."

I compliment Holbrook on doing a bang-up job of framing me and he graciously accepts the earnest praise.

"While we both know full well that you were not in fact responsible for Mister Zimmerman's death, the fact that two weapons registered in your name were used in the shooting and the fact that you were seen in the vicinity of ChumSpot Headquarters at the time of the murder is a rather alarming amount of circumstantial evidence that even the most inept of District Attorneys would likely be able to parlay into a conviction. There's a chance this evidence can be usurped however."

I've got no idea what Holbrook is getting at so I ask him and he tells me to be patient. His thug repeats his boss' instructions almost verbatim.

"The possibility currently exists," Holbrook announces, "for me to arrange for the fingerprints of the man *actually* responsible for Mister Zimmerman's untimely demise to be placed upon the handle of your Desert Eagle, which we kept for…let's say… sentimental reasons…"

The narrator lets us know that the corpses of Holbrook's dead henchmen are being held at some private underground morgue owned by Tetrace. Apparently they'd somehow beaten the authorities to the cul-de-sac in Peoria, cleaned up the crime scene and taken the bodies.

Holbrook takes his gloves off. "So. Shane. What I'm prepared to offer you is this—in the event that you do a satisfactory job of the assignment we're going to be charging you with, we will have the guilty party's fingerprints placed upon this second gun, which we will proceed to submit to the police along with the bodies of both of the real assassins and a camera phone video of them committing the crime. You'll immediately be cleared of all wrong-doing, be able to move back into that shithole of an apartment you call home and go back to playing cards, drinking heavily, and abusing various narcotics in what I'm sure you deem to be a recreational manner. So. What do you say?"

I've obviously got no other choice but to accept but I act like this is a negotiation and demand to know the details of this assignment he's talking about. Holbrook takes a sheet of paper out of his back pocket, unfolds it, and hands it to me after giving it a quick once-over. I inspect the sheet and it's a list of website URLs, most of which I recognize.

"You of course remember that fake computer virus you convinced poor Mister Daniels to upload onto our system a few weeks back?"

A nuclear explosion goes off inside my head as I finally realize that Holbrook must've been Dave's contact at Tetrace—the one who'd been giving us so much business. I ask Holbrook about it and he just smiles widely and gives me an expressive wink, confirming my suspicions. My body temperature is starting to approach critical levels, my heart pumping liquid hot magma.

"And you set that fire at Sancus to cover your tracks didn't you? I should kill you right now you piece of shit!" I make a move towards Holbrook but the Aussie grabs me by both arms and puts me in some kind of wrestling hold that I can't even struggle against. Fuck.

"You're in no position to make threats I'm afraid," Holbrook announces. "Quite the opposite in fact. At any rate, what's done is done—there's no use in crying over spilled milk now is there, Shane?"

My jaw's clenched more firmly than I'd ever thought possible and I'm too upset to speak. Holbrook decides to interpret my silence as a reluctant acceptance of his logic. Bastard.

"Now, getting back to the assignment..." Holbrook begins pacing around the room like an effete army officer. "The virus implanted upon the flash disc Daniels was given was in fact quite real. We finished development on it earlier this year and have been extremely pleased with its results."

"So you want me to install it at each of these websites to shut them down and give you assholes even more control of the internet?"

Holbrook claps his hands together in delight. He congratulates me on my successful guess in an 'overtly theatrical' manner. "Your new friend down in Arizona can probably take care of most of those sites vis-à-vis his world-class hacking skills. His involvement obviously won't get back to us so we're fine with it. A couple of them, however, will need to be taken care of manually, 'up close and personal' as they say—a task that will require your unique skills set, Officer. So. There's the deal. You take care of this for us and we'll turn in the evidence which clears your name. Agreed?"

I hate myself for making the deal but I do it. Frederick slaps me on the back and welcomes me to the team as Holbrook giddily proclaims that he loves it when two parties can put aside their animosity in order to complete an agreement which is mutually advantageous. He uses really flowery language and the narrator even makes fun of him for sounding like a homo.

«««—»»»

The guy sitting next to me on my flight back to Phoenix has an old-fashioned Discman with him and his gigantic binder of CDs barely fits beneath the seat in front of him. I ask him if he's a time traveler from the year 1995 and he laughs and tells me that he hates mp3 players because they're a 'betrayal of the art form.' I immediately regret it when I ask him what he means and he lectures me for twenty minutes about how music is meant to be consumed by listeners in a structured, predetermined manner which is 'inherently finite.'

According to my fellow southbound traveler, modern digital music devices don't effectively convey the artistry of their medium for several reasons, one of which is the absence of any physical representation of the music like there was with LPs, tapes, etc. which I don't really get but whatever. Plus he doesn't like that, in this digital age, songs can be rearranged in any order the listener sees fit and playlists can be made that could theoretically go on forever in an 'infinite gestation loop.' Okay. "Albums should have a beginning, middle, and an end," he tells me, a noble passion resonating in his voice. "Just like life."

I let the conversation end momentarily, charitably giving the moron a few seconds of silence to make it seem like the semi-profound statement he's just made is some kind of revelation. Fuck it. *Let him have it.*

"That's bullshit," I tell him. "Life isn't some contrived, pre-packaged, easy-to-follow-along piece of art. It's a long, arbitrary, circuitous journey to nowhere. Get off your wallet and buy a fucking zPod already."

The guy kind of just snickers and puts his massive headphones on. I pretend that I'm asleep for a while and then I am.

«««—»»»

Once my cab is completely out of sight I walk up to The Wizard's trailer and it takes a while for him to lower me down into his bunker. I catch myself struggling to ward off an encroaching sense of dread.

The Wizard's slouched in his gigantic chair in a position that looks wholly uncomfortable. He looks utterly crestfallen. His homely complexion is buried beneath an avalanche of paleness and his eyes are bloodshot to hell. "So I guess you had an interesting trip, huh Shane?" he asks in what can barely be classified a murmur.

"Yeah, I guess you could say that. How's your week been?"

In a 'peculiar, soporific' voice the Wizard tells me that as soon as he established a link with Tetrace's mainframe on the remote server he gave me, they hijacked his system with some kind of overdrive program that immediately stole all of his computer files. Then he tells me that they installed a delayed-response virus in his mainframe that will completely wipe out everything on there in two weeks unless he helps me take their competitors offline. He's tried to circumvent it but that hasn't proven successful and he explains it all to me using his bullshit technobabble words and I don't have a clue what any of it means but I guess overall it's bad. "The Sword of Damocles is dangling over us, partner. I suppose I really should've known better than to mess with Tetrace."

I walk over to The Wizard's perch and do my best to sound enthusiastic about the whole thing. "Listen, man, it's no big deal. We just do the job like they say and then it'll all be over. You get your system back and I get my life back." I hand over the sheet of paper Holbrook gave in San Jose. "I'm sure it's a piece of cake to pull off for ya. You can hack into these sites and shut them down in five seconds, right?"

The Wizard sighs and tells me he can easily shut down six of the nine sites they desperately want to embarrass: MyPlace, TuneMaster, JizzSpot, Yeehaw!, BlogCentral, and Gregslist. *Gregslist? Seriously??* I look at the sheet me and take inventory of the three I'll apparently have to infiltrate somehow in order to facilitate a manual shutdown.

"So that leaves Bleep, PokerSphere, and…CumSpot?"

The Wizard's silent for a few seconds, seemingly lost deep in thought. "Yeah," he eventually groans. "I can't get those three—their firewalls are too sophisticated. You'll have to break into their headquarters and upload the virus manually, or somehow swipe one of their webmasters' token key fobs that automatically delivers a new, unique access code every sixty seconds. Either way it won't be easy, Shane."

"None of these companies are on Tetrace's level though, right? Just a porn site, a poker site, and some new search engine?"

The Wizard explains to me that PokerSphere is based on a Native American Reservation in upstate New York. CumSpot is one of the only porn sites still making money since they produce all of their material in-house and use a new video streaming technique that makes it impossible to duplicate their content, for the time being at least. "Both of those setups are a bit tricky but shouldn't be impossible to take out," he says.

"What about Bleep?"

"That's going to be a tough cookie to crack. They're owned and operated by MetroTech." After reading my blank expression for a moment he sighs and continues. "MetroTech is a massive hardware manufacturer that's been making waves on the web frontier as of late, reinvesting all the profits from their zPad and zPhone sales into becoming a major player in the online world. Bleep was launched as a direct competitor to Tetrace's flagship site but so far it hasn't made much noise despite some extremely aggressive traditional and viral marketing efforts. At any rate, to answer your question, yes, their security might be close to Tetrace's level."

The narrator's arguing with his editor about 'showing versus telling' in his text and their squabble lasts for a pretty long time. "Well then," I announce after they finally finish. "I guess we'll have to be careful then, won't we?"

We search every job site on the net but we can't find any openings at Bleep, MetroTech, or any of its umbrella companies. *Stupid recession*. After a brief discussion we decide that I'll just show up at their corporate headquarters in Oklahoma, claim to be an IRS agent, and demand to speak with their comptroller. The

Wizard seems to think that there'll be a few minutes where I'll able to sneak into an office and install the virus while they're trying checking my credentials and figuring out what to do with me when they discover I'm bogus. "That's a long enough window for you to do your thing." I can't quite place his latest register, nor can I come up with a better plan so I agree to go along with it. It's completely ridiculous but that's never stopped me before, plus it seems like it'll be an entertaining ride for all of us.

The Wizard sets me up with all kinds of legitimate-looking pieces of identification for "IRS Investigator Terry Brelen," complete with a cool badge he produces on a machine that looks like it belongs in the background of some cheesy fantasy movie. He uses Terry's brand spanking new credit card to book me a bus ticket to Oklahoma City and a rental car for when I get there. I protest and ask why I can't fly and he tells me that it'll be too difficult for me/Terry to get through airport security.

"And why is that?" I ask.

"Because. You're definitely going to want to have a gun with you when you show up at MetroTech on Friday. A big one."

«««—»»»

I meet Roger at a tavern we used to go to all the time back when we were on the force together. Now he owns it. We down a couple of beers and talk about the Cardinals for a bit before discussing the lunacy surrounding my life at the moment. I'm sure things in Roger's world are pretty crazy as well but I don't ask him any details since I don't really care. He casually hands me a large, heavy paper bag and I stash it under my chair for the moment.

"Thanks man," I say. "I owe you."

"You don't owe me nothing," Roger proclaims. "I could give you a million guns and we wouldn't be even, not by a long shot."

I'm not exactly sure what I'd do with a million guns but I thank him again and take a sip of beer. The narrator takes his sweet ass time explaining how I'd saved Roger's life once by pulling him out of a burning car after we'd been ambushed by a bunch of spic gangbangers at the zenith of the race riots. We just missed being blown to bits by a second or two and I guess if I'd had more time to think about it I probably wouldn't have even tried to save him. Whatever.

«««—»»»

They show us a bunch of shitty movies during our twenty-hour bus ride to Oklahoma City, which at least makes the time pass by pretty quickly I guess. The first flick is about a high school in suburban Connecticut where somebody spray paints a swastika onto a Jewish kid's locker. This young, leggy bombshell of a principal has to deal with all kinds of bullshit from the PTA, minority rights groups, and nosy reporters while she investigates the incident. The twist at the end is that the kid vandalized his own locker so that anti-Semitism would appear to be more prominent than other kinds of racism in their school and he'd get to feel special about being persecuted and shit, making him more important than his black, Asian, and Hispanic friends in his fucked-up mind.

After that they show us an action movie called FROST BITE about terrorists taking over the Winter Olympics in France. The hero—an American tourist whose name just happens to be Michael Frost—has to take the bad guys out one-by-one all through the Olympic Village and he gives a clever one-liner every time he kills a terrorist. When he decapitates a guy with a super-sharp sled he goes: "I win. You luge!" Then he stabs a guy through the heart with the pointy end of a ski pole and says: "Ski you in hell!" In the end the main villain, who I think is supposed to be German but the actor does an awful job on the accent, is getting away on a snowmobile and Frost has to shoot him with a sniper rifle after cross-country skiing for a long time. After he fires his shot and the snowmobile blows up he quips: "America takes Gold in the biathlon."

When FROST BITE wraps up they throw on this retarded romantic comedy where a super hot twenty-something urbanite inherits her estranged father's plantation in the Deep South. She ends up falling in love with one of the farmhands and they have to raise a bunch of money to save the ranch from evil bankers or something.

Up next is THE PTOLEMY ENIGMA which is based upon a best-selling book I never got around to reading. In the movie version some scientist is scrambling to find an ancient scroll that this famous Roman astrologist wrote out with all of the constellations on it because there's some astrological crisis approaching and only by finding the coordinates of a mysterious forgotten star cluster can Earth be saved from disaster. I don't understand a goddamn word in the thing but in the end the scientist indeed finds the scroll and manages to save the world from celestial destruction in the nick of time. Phew.

The last movie they show us is some bullshit art-house junk that's shot all in black and white. I fall asleep twenty minutes into it and have a pretty crazy dream where I'm sailing towards the edge of the world in a one-man schooner.

«««—»»»

The receptionist at MetroTech's Oklahoma City branch is a big fat black chick that has one of those Africanized-sounding names that I don't even attempt to pronounce. There are no fewer than four aquariums in the building's marble-floored lobby and I try not to stare at the gnarly neon fish as I wait for a senior member of their accounting team to respond to a page. Moeshaliquaballa or whatever her name is asks me to take a seat and I tell her I'd prefer to stand, which the narrator thinks is a shrewd decision that emphasizes my character's 'ardent humorlessness.'

After spending a few minutes standing around looking official and shit a portly Arabic-looking guy in a poorly-cut suit shows up with a security guard and introduces himself as MetroTech Vice President of Finance Omar Maroush. He asks to see my credentials. I hand over my fake IRS badge and tell him I have a few questions about their most recent tax return and he seems to be extremely suspicious about the whole thing. He asks me to follow him after a tense, silent moment.

The security guard shadows me as we make our way through an opulent office complex, up to the twenty-second floor where the accounting department is apparently located. I'm made to wait in an empty white room while Maroush retrieves the relevant data pertaining to my surprise visit. A barrel-chested MetroTech sentinel stands at the door. He tucks his hands behind his back formally, as if he's standing watch at some fancy European palace.

I ask the guard if I can use the bathroom. He grunts and escorts me down a long hallway to an immaculate lavatory that the term 'luxury' doesn't do justice. As soon as we walk in I hammer the guard in the chin with my right elbow and whirl around to catch him with a left cross that knocks him out immediately. I drag his unconscious body into a bathroom stall and prop him up atop an impeccably well-maintained porcelain toilet.

The adrenaline's pumping through me pretty good now and my pulse is racing as I leave the bathroom and scour the hallway for a vacant office. I finally find one and within a few seconds I've uploaded Tetrace's virus onto its desktop. I yank the flash disc out of the data port and walk briskly back towards the elevator. Maroush spots me and yells at my back. When I don't respond he yells again and the elevator's still a dozen floors away according to the electronic readout thingy so I dart onto the stairwell and sprint back down towards the lobby taking four steps at a time.

When I reach the ground floor there's a pair of security agents waiting for me and after I kick the first one in the balls the second one wraps me up in a bear hug. He's a big burly motherfucker but when I slam the back of my head into his nose he lets me go and I give him a karate chop to the temple that should give him a concussion or maybe worse.

I make it out of the front doors and when I look back at the building I see a several more security guards chasing after me. I spin around and tear open my briefcase in a single, fluid motion. I rip the pistol Roger gave me out if its Velcro casing and fire a bunch of warning shots over the assholes' heads. They immediately drop to the ground and begin clumsily fumbling for their weapons in unison, as if the whole thing's been meticulously choreographed by some Hollywood stunt coordinator. By the time they're back on their feet I'm speeding away in my rental car.

As far as I can tell they don't even bother pursuing me, probably due to some bullshit union protocol or something. Once I get on the highway I decide pretty quickly that I should forget about the return portion of my bus ticket and just drive myself back to Phoenix. The narrator's surprisingly flattering as he relays his account of my mindset at the moment.

Terry Brelen's rental came equipped with a bitchin' satellite radio and I listen to a 24-hours-a-day news channel for most of my drive home because it's a good distraction and I'm not in the mood for any bullshit music. The mid-term senatorial elections are today and a bunch of assholes I've never heard of are either winning or losing all over the country.

After a few minutes I remember what The Wizard told me about how the fate of the Tetrace Corporation could very well be determined by the outcome of this thing so then I pay attention as best I can. The main newscaster's a woman that sounds pretty sexy so it's not too bad I guess.

"Our commercial-free coverage of the mid-term elections continues," she tells me in her sultry bedroom voice. "And we are now able to confirm a pair of shocking upsets. Georgia's Vance Turner and Ohio's Michael Fulton have both been defeated despite owning double-digit leads in the polls in the days leading up to this evening's election. Both incumbent candidates' campaigns were evidently quite badly damaged by false rumors of sexual deviance which spread like wildfire via social networking sites such as

THE SPARTAK TRIGGER

ChumSpot and Chirrup throughout the afternoon. An entry at both politicians' infopedia pages even contained information about the fabricated incidents for a few hours earlier today, with hundreds of thousands of residents of both states having been exposed to these completely untrue allegations."

I pull over to the side of the road and crank the volume on the satellite radio up as high as it'll go. The woman explains that photographs of both devoutly Christian candidates posing in Nazi uniforms with scantily-clad teenaged girls at some S&M nightclub had circulated throughout the internet all day. Apparently by the time the mainstream media got a hold of the story and determined that the pictures had been doctored, the damage had already been done.

"Coincidentally," the hot-sounding broad continues, "a record number of identity theft cases have been reported in both states in the last forty-eight hours, a trend which led to a record low voter turnout as victims of this alarmingly widespread scam were unable to properly register at polling stations."

"That's no coincidence," I announce. The narrator immediately starts making fun of me for talking to myself. Fair enough.

The Wizard's hands are shaking like a degenerate alcoholic with Parkinson's disease. He's not really making any sense as he tries to tell me what the hell happened with this election shit. After I get right up in his face and scream for him to get it together he takes several deep puffs from his asthma inhaler and manages to compose himself.

"They used *my* program!" he yelps, indignantly. "My identity theft algorithm—those bastards must've stolen it from my system when they hijacked me the other day. The Wizard and narrator take turns explaining how Tetrace uploaded the deceptively-complex algorithm onto targeted ChumSpot subscribers' accounts and used the information on there to figure out online banking passwords and shit from various profile elements—

birthdays, favorite movies, high school friends' nicknames, etc. "It took me three goddamn *years* to develop write that code, and now those assholes at Tetrace have it!"

I ask The Wizard how exactly he knows that it was *his* program that Tetrace used to orchestrate the genocidal identity theft campaign that apparently helped rig a pair of elections. He once again mumbles through a bunch of technobabble that makes absolutely no sense to me but I just keep nodding and that seems to calm him down for some reason. Thankfully, the narrator surmises everything he's saying in a really straightforward manner that I can actually follow. When he's done I take a seat next to The Wizard and ask him if he's got any booze. He apologizes for not having any and we sit in similar poses expressing our mutual dejection for a while.

"Maybe this was their plan all along," I hear myself say after a couple of minutes.

"What do you mean?" The Wizard snivels.

"Maybe that's what Tetrace wanted this whole time—to steal your identity theft program after they acquired ChumSpot to use it for this thing. They obviously knew I was a friend of Roger's and they also probably knew that you work for him. Maybe they set me up just so I'd end up going to Roger for help, which they knew would lead them to you."

"Jesus," The Wizard says softly, a faint look of excitement ebbing over his gaunt face. "And here I thought *I* was the paranoid one…"

«««—»»»

I go to visit Iris but she's not home. Her roommate tells me she's gone to Chicago to appear on some TV show. I ask the bitch what show it is and she tells me to fuck off and slams the door in my face. Then I go to a pet store and ask the friendly salespeople all kinds of retarded questions but I don't buy anything.

THE SPARTAK TRIGGER

《《《—》》》

The latest identity The Wizard's hooked me up with is that of an out-of-work, second-rate 'erotic film' director named Jack Stone. He seems to know a hell of a lot about the porn industry and tells me exactly what to say and how to act when I visit Aphrodite Enterprises' head office. The Wizard even gives me a DVD of some 'SUPER hot' scenes I'm supposed to have shot recently. When I ask him where he got it he abruptly changes the subject and mutters something about Pangaea in a queer singsong voice.

《《《—》》》

I walk through the front doors at Aphrodite Enterprises, Inc. and 'assertively bound' over to the receptionist. She's got perky, fake tits that a low-cut blouse showcases perfectly. They distract me for a second but then I'm back in character and I ask the slut in my fake southern accent if I can talk to the head producer about showing him my demo reel and getting a job making movies for CumSpot.

"You'll have to make an appointment," she tells me in an irritatingly high-pitched voice. I almost tell her to lay off the helium after I sign up to see some guy called David O'Sellsdick in the morning but then I don't. I bump into a linebacker-sized shithead on my way out of the building and he tells me to watch where I'm going. Then he corrects himself and says I should watch where *he's* going. I somehow manage to stay in character and apologize, keeping the rage surging through me in check just long enough to make it to my rental car where I unleash a bombardment of anger upon a surprisingly forgiving dash board. I wipe the blood off of my hands and drive back to my motel.

《《《—》》》

The broad sitting alone at a table across from me looks really familiar. She's not wearing much makeup but she's got a specific, skanky look to her that makes me think she might be a hooker I used to bang or something. She catches me staring at her and asks me politely if I want an autograph. I tell her no and she says I should leave her alone then, curtly.

I turn my attention back to the ball game I've been watching and then I realize that she's a veteran porn actress that I've jerked off to quite a few times over the years. Against my better judgment I stand up and walk over to get a closer look at Ms. Taylor de Maumaront.

"What do you want, old man?" she demands. "I thought you said you didn't want my autograph. You gonna try and pick me up then? Is that it? You want to try and fuck me, Numbnuts?"

I tell her I just wanted to buy her a drink and that I was staring at her earlier because I was blown away that such a beautiful woman could be sitting alone at such a shitty bar. The narrator tells me I'm acting quite 'debonair' so good for me I guess. She laughs drunkenly and tells me to get her a double rum and cola, hold the cola.

The bartender gives me a 'derisive' look when I place the order and I tell him to perk up when he hands me the drinks. Taylor asks me what we should drink to and I tell her America and she tells me she's got two brothers fighting overseas so I say that's all the more reason to drink to our great nation. We clink glasses and each take generous swigs.

"Yeah, the U.S. may be fucked up as fuck but it's still the best damn country in the world," Taylor says. She's fumbling with her words as she speaks and my dick starts to get hard when I realize just how hammered she is. I nod and ask her if she's actually famous, playing dumb.

"Yeah, I'm famous," she says, flashing a 'coquettish' smile. "I'm an actress dude. Adult entertainment. With Aphrodite Films."

"That's very interesting." I notice a freshish bruise on Taylor's neck when she fiddles with her long black hair. She's got to be at least forty-five I guess but she definitely doesn't look it. The narrator gives us a *completely* unnecessary backstory about our new minor character, going into painfully-excessive detail about Taylor's pseudotragic upbringing—broken home, sexually abusive uncle, crystal meth addiction, and so on and so forth. I play an invisible violin and Taylor asks me what the hell I'm doing. "Sorry," I say, 'diffidently.' "I've got a really weird strand of Tourette's Syndrome."

After a few more drinks I confess to Taylor that I did recognize her earlier from a videotape I owned back in the nineties. A look of savage glee comes upon her face after I make this revelation. "I haven't really gotten into this whole online thing though," I tell her, trying to redirect the conversation. "No offense—I'm sure the pay's pretty decent in internet porn and all. It's just not my cup of tea."

Taylor chortles boisterously for what feels like a long time. After she calms herself down from the frantic laugh attack she tells me that the internet's ruining all of society, starting with her industry. I ask her to explain.

"At first, yeah, it was great," she says, beginning her lecture with the enthusiasm of a garrulous sailor. "Lots more work, lots more companies that all paid pretty well… Then all the upstart operations went under and there were all of these extra performers competing for fewer and fewer jobs, doing more fucked up shit for less and less money." There's a jarring, barren hush for a moment as Taylor carefully collects her drunken thoughts.

She goes on to explain how there's so much free, high-quality porn available on the internet now that there are only a handful of companies making any money, and their profit margins are razor thin. Aphrodite is one of them (mainly because they've diversified and now, in addition to literally hundreds of porn sites, run a highly-successful online dating service that arranges for married people to have affairs amongst a variety of other morally-questionable enterprises), but that will only last so long.

I make a joke about a government bailout but she doesn't seem to hear me. Taylor bitterly states that it's just a matter of time before this happens to every form of art, using impressive-sounding phrases like 'commoditization of culture' and 'toxic placebo.' She says that people are downloading everything for free now—books, TV shows, movies, etc.—meaning that less and less money will be allocated to production and therefore quality will ultimately deteriorate dramatically.

When I tell Taylor that porn's different than mainstream culture she doesn't like it. Not at all. "Everything's a form of pornography when you think about it," she pleads. "Sitcoms, theme parks, romantic comedies. They offer, like, an idealized escape from existence, y'know? A straightforward fantasy that's nothing at all like real life." I think I understand the point she's making. The narrator excitedly chimes in and mentions that while all of this is happening, websites like WatchThis.com are shortening peoples' attention spans down to microscopic levels, inadvertently lowering our collective IQ and enhancing a 'primitive need for immediacy' that will soon reach critical levels.

Then the narrator and Taylor start speaking in unison about how the way people communicate nowadays is 'high-tech primitiveness on steroids.' They say that texting and instant messaging and shit have reduced peoples' vocabularies into a series of ridiculous acronyms and nonsensical slang terms and that smartphones have cultivated a culture where direct human interaction is avoided at every opportunity. "Eventually we won't even speak to one another at all," they say. "We'll be connected by some high-tech conduit and that'll be how we reproduce too in a hundred years or so, while watching virtual porn probably." I tell them we're starting to get a bit preachy here and they both tell me to shut the fuck up. They tell us humanity's never been closer but further apart as a species and blah blah blah. I'm not sure that that any of this makes any sense but whatever. I don't really care either way.

I ask Taylor how she knows so much about technology and shit from acting in porn and she tells me that she doesn't really do that anymore. "I went back to school a few years back and got my degree in computer science," she says. "I'm the web manager at Aphrodite now actually. Too old to do much acting anymore."

"Interesting," I say. "Very interesting indeed."

"Yeah, once you hit forty in this business the demand for your talents starts to fade pretty fast." Taylor's biting her lower lip hard and I notice that her eyes are starting to glaze over so I tell her we should leave. I help her stand up and we take a cab back to my motel. When I can't get it up I just pull her hair and do some other violent stuff for a while, which she seems to enjoy.

«««—»»»

A violent nightmare wakes me up at 3:54am and I stagger into the bathroom and splash some cold water on my face. I knock Taylor's purse over when I reach for a towel and a bunch of shit falls out, including an electronic doohickey that looks like it could be one of the code readout token key fobs that Wiz told me about. Sweet. I quickly shovel everything else back into the tattered handbag and I text Wiz to see if he's awake and of course he is so I send keep sending him the codes as they pop up on the digital readout thingy.

The Wizard eventually tells me we're good to go so I put the fob back in Taylor's purse and climb back into bed with her. I wrap my arms around her and whisper that I love her and pray to god that this is real but it seems like that's not possible. The narrator tells me this is the happiest I'll ever be for the rest of my life and I thank him for letting me know even though that completely ruins the moment.

«««—»»»

On my way back to Phoenix I stop and sleep for a day-and-a-half straight at some bed and breakfast in central Nevada. When

I wake up I turn on the TV and see my daughter on the set of a daytime talk show hosted by Patty Summers. Iris is introduced by Ms. Summers as a soon-to-be-mother who's looking to find out who the father of her unborn child is.

The narrator tells me I've never been more furious in my life as a glowing red tinge flanks the edges of my line of sight. I stand up and grip the sides of the TV with a pair of badly-shaking hands. A warm fluid starts dripping down my face and I don't even have to check to know that it's blood.

Patty brings out not one, not two, not three, but FOUR dudes and they each tell the story about when and where they banged Iris. Before she can read the results of the paternity test I've smashed the TV onto the ground and watched myself completely trash my room. The nice elderly couple that owns the place calls the cops but I'm back on the road before they arrive.

<<<—>>>

I visit Roger at one of his clubs and he's counting a mountain of cash in the back room. He tells me that he doesn't trust any of his underlings to handle the accounting at this particular venue so he does it all himself. I tell him that I'm impressed even though I couldn't care less.

After he's done we go out to the main bar area and Roger grabs us a couple of beers. I ask him if he'd seen the Patty Summers Show lately and he laughs and makes fun of some fat baby that was on there the other day. "No, that's not the episode I'm talking about," I say. "Iris was on there this afternoon trying to figure out who the fucking father of her kid is."

Roger grimaces at the news of his goddaughter's embarrassing appearance on syndicated television and offers me his condolences as he breaks out a massive bag of weed. He starts to roll a joint on a silvery bar top that looks like it belongs in another decade—either the 1970's or 2130's. I start to tell Roger about how I'd pretended to be a porn director up in Oregon and shit but he ignores me as an expression of 'profound gravity' marches across his face.

"It's been a rough week, partner," Roger grunts. I don't respond. He goes on to tell me all about how some big mafia boss from out east has been trying to break into the human smuggling game and has been giving his people lots of problems at the border. "They've been giving these crazy rednecks all kinds of badass weaponry to fire at our convoys. I lost three shipments and four soldiers this morning, dude."

"That sucks, man," I offer. For some reason the narrator compares our fraternal ambivalence to the kind of detached intimacy propagated by social networking websites like ChumSpot and I think to myself that 'intimate detachment' might've sounded better but I guess it doesn't really matter. Roger finally finishes rolling the joint but then we realize that neither one of us has a lighter.

«««—»»»

The lineup at the deli isn't all that long but the cashier and the two idiots making sandwiches are slow as handicapped molasses and I'm starting to get pretty fucking antsy from a combination of hunger and impatience. A couple of Jewish-looking teenaged bitches cut to the front of the line as soon as they walk into the place and when someone says something to them about it they insist they're just getting a bottle of water but then one of them decides to get a tuna-on-rye and the joint's dimwitted employees oblige her while everyone else in line lets out a collective groan. I fondle the keys in my pocket and think about rushing forward and stabbing each of the sluts in the throat with one of them but then I decide not to.

«««—»»»

The Wizard looks like he's been awake for three straight weeks. A massive pile of empty energy drink cans surrounding him adds credence to this notion. He's been going on about some crazy theory of his involving cryptic messages appearing on Chirrup for about ten minutes now and his temperament is bordering upon outright lunacy.

"Then there's this chirp from Cool Guy Ninety-One," he says, his voice teeming with frenzy. "'Going to movies later. Any suggestions?' He gets a re-chirp from Cool Guy Seventeen, and then Man of Steel Fifty-Three double replies to both of them that 'October Companion' is a great flick and that he's going to see it again soon and, get this, the message has a hash-marked ARPA next to it!"

"So fucking what?"

"Don't you see??" The Wizard pleads. "Seventeen was the year of the Russian Revolution. Ninety-one is the year the Soviet Union collapsed. 'Man of Steel' was the nickname of Stalin, who was head of the USSR until Nineteen Fifty-Three. Plus, the Russian translation of 'Companion' is 'Sputnik,' which the Soviets launched in October of Nineteen Fifty-Seven and caused the Americans to develop the Advanced Research Projects Agency, or 'ARPA,' All the pieces fit together perfectly!"

"Plus the weather's not exactly tropical in Russia, so that would explain the 'cool guy' monikers, right?" I guess The Wizard doesn't pick up on my mockery because he goes on to explain his theory in its entirety, something about neo-Bolshevik computer hackers and subliminal messages being implanted throughout the internet. I seem to understand what he's saying a lot better than the narrator does, which is somewhat unsettling. "What does it all mean though?" I ask. "What's this alleged conspiracy's end game?"

The Wizard pauses for a moment before admitting that he's not entirely sure.

"Look, this is all extremely interesting, Wiz, but we've still got one more assignment to complete for Tetrace you realize."

"About that." The Wizard turns to face me and his skeletal facial features seem almost cartoonlike in the vibrant glow of his futuristic computer station. "I've been doing some thinking and I really don't believe that Tetrace is likely to fulfill the promises they've made us should we indeed finish taking their competitors offline."

I know The Wizard's 100% right on this one but I haven't figured out any other way to get us out of the mess we're in so I pretend that I trust Holbrook implicitly and reassure my partner in crime that we'll be indeed be rewarded for our actions. The narrator expounds my performance in an overtly sardonic manner. Bastard. "We've just gotta roll with the plot, that's how these things go, right?"

Suddenly brimming with constructive rationality, The Wizard tells me we need to somehow have a card up our sleeves to play in the highly-likely event that Tetrace indeed double-crosses us and still ruins his computer system while destroying the evidence that would clear me of all charges in the Zimmerman murder. "What'd you have in mind?" I ask.

He says we should investigate both the Daniels suicide and the Jennings murder, to see if we can dig up anything that implicates Holbrook directly in the two deaths somehow. "You never know." He sounds like a hard-boiled detective from some old black-and-white pulp serial. "They may have left a vital piece of evidence behind that we can use against them. Nobody's perfect after all." I feel stupid for not having thought of this before but I guess you'd need a paranoid brain like The Wizard's got to reverse engineer a plan like this.

We're way ahead of schedule on the Tetrace operation so I tell The Wizard to look into it, as if I'm the one in charge here. He says he already has. Shocking.

"Okay then, what'd ya dig up, Weird Science?"

The Wizard waits a while before responding, ostensibly gathering his thoughts. "Well, Olivia Jennings' murder is still being investigated by authorities," he states gravely. "And, according to my research…Archie Daniels is still alive."

«‹‹—››»

Iris takes a long time to answer her door after I bang on it forcefully with firmly-clenched fists. There's liquor on her breath when she welcomes me into her filth-ridden apartment.

"You should really think about using that money I gave you to hire a cleaning lady," I tell her.

"Yeah, that's a good idea, pops."

I tell Iris I saw her on the Patty Summers show. She snickers and claims she knew full well that none of those guys had knocked her up. She'd just wanted a free trip to Chicago so she lied to the producers. I turn to face her and demand to know who the father of my grandchild is immediately. She says it doesn't matter anymore.

"What do you mean?" I hear myself yell. Iris lifts her shirt to show off her flat belly and explains that she had a miscarriage. The narrator's voice quivers slightly as he relays certain aspects of the scene while omitting others. He probably thinks I'm going to do something awful, which I did in an earlier draft, but I just end up breaking down and crying now while Iris laughs at me cruelly, calling me a loser.

I've never felt so hopeless or pathetic in my life but I somehow manage to regain a modicum of composure and tell my daughter that I know I've made a ton of mistakes in my life and have a lot to answer for when my time comes but she still means everything to me and all I want in the world is for her to be happy. That makes her stop laughing at me then we kind of just stand there for a while, not really sure what we're supposed to do as the callous caress of regret continues to molest us both for quite some time.

«««—»»»

Silverman Chase's head of security is a huge moron and he doesn't really question me when I tell him I'm a private eye whose been hired by Olivia Jennings' family to investigate her still-unsolved murder. He lets me interview her coworkers, who've all been interrogated by Seattle's finest already. They keep telling me how weird it is to be answering the same questions again and they all seem to think that Jennings' murder was tied in with her cocaine problem. Every time someone mentions her specious addiction I have to suppress a smile.

The last person I talk to is Jennings' boss. His last name is Chase so I assume his grandfather cofounded the company with Silverman, who was either gay or didn't produce any worthwhile heirs since no one with that surname is in the company directory. Oh well.

I can somehow tell by the way Chase eyeballs me when I enter his office that he knew all about the arrangement his company made with Sancus and doesn't like having me here, not one bit. I introduce myself—well, myself as Ryan Butler—and we shake hands like we're athletes on rival teams at the start of a championship series. Chase looks like he's in pretty good shape for a pampered trust fund faggot. He probably has a high-end personal trainer or something. His expensive clothes and designer tie all project an image of unimaginable affluence but there's a primal, animalistic quality about him that makes me think he's into some pretty messed up shit away from the office.

"The police were here about a month ago, Mister Butler." His tone is blustery, arrogant. "We were quite cooperative with their investigation."

Some broad with a huge ass brings me a bottle of something called Apollinaris. Chase insists upon giving me a lime. I try not to look at his assistant's spacious backyard as she leaves but I can't help myself.

"I'm sure you were indeed accommodating to local law enforcement Mister Chase, but, as you know, Miss Jennings' killers have not yet been brought to justice." I pretend to cough for some reason. "As such, her family decided to procure my services to ensure that due diligence has been followed, and that no stone has been left unturned."

"I didn't realize that Olivia had any family. She told us that her parents died in a car crash when she was a teenager." Chase's eyebrows are raised expectantly and he's looking at me with focused, accusatory eyes. Without hesitation I explain to him that I was hired by Annette Jennings, Olivia's step-aunt who lives in Illinois and was her legal guardian for a time. He seems to buy it.

"What can you tell me about Miss Jennings?" I ask.

The clean-cut millionaire sighs expressively and leans back in his chair. He gives me a fiery-yet-pensive look, like he's trying to get a read on me and we're playing a stratagem-based board game, which I guess we are.

"Well?" I ask, blithely.

He sighs again and tells me that Olivia was a classic workaholic. Her job was everything to her. She didn't date, didn't have any hobbies. She didn't do much of anything besides worry about 'the market,' 'the Dow,' shit like that.

"Too bad—hot piece of ass like that," I hear myself say. I can't tell if this was part of my inner monologue or not but Chase is giving me a weird look like I said it aloud. Oh well. I ask him if Olivia had any enemies that he knew of and he says there were too many to list. I ask him what he means and he looks at me like I've got six heads.

"Don't you know?" the prick asks me in a psychondescending (sic) manner. "She really pissed a lot of people off during the subprime mortgage crisis. Powerful people. People I wouldn't want to be on the bad side of." I act like I know what he's talking about for a minute or so and then awkwardly try and prod him about Olivia's apparently-shady dealings. The narrator's outright insulting my complete lack of finesse the whole time and I have to use up a huge amount of mental energy just trying to ignore him.

Then it hits me. "So why didn't you take any action against Ms. Chase after all of these dissatisfied clients came forward?" I ask after taking a sip of water. Chase's eyes bulge out of his head the instant the words leave my mouth but then he composes himself a split-second later and leans in towards me. "We couldn't," he hisses. "She had a very…favorable employment contract."

I let this revelation hang unpleasantly in the air for a moment, like a used condom half-filled with helium. "What about this arrest for cocaine possession that took place shortly before her disappearance?" I ask, defiantly. "Did anyone here have any idea she was involved with narcotics at all?"

"Absolutely not," Chase grunts. "We have a zero-tolerance policy when it comes to that sort of thing. Our employees undergo regular drug testing so if she'd been using that stuff for a while she was also somehow cheating the tests. The investment business is extremely competitive Mister Butler. I can tell you quite plainly that clients don't want to have to worry about their advisors being in anything less than a lucid state when they're making such life-altering decisions."

"I bet her arrest would've given you grounds to terminate her contract no questions asked though, am I right?"

Chase takes a deep breath and acknowledges that their legal department had already begun making arrangements to do exactly that when Jennings' body had been discovered in the trunk of a car. "She was to be terminated that very afternoon," he admits, even choking up a bit. *This guy is good.*

"Well I guess someone beat you to it," I quip, coldly.

Chase responds almost immediately, as if he's rehearsed this exchange beforehand somehow: "Yes, well, the drug-dealing business is one of the few industries more ruthless and volatile than our own. It would appear she'd angered the wrong people in that arena as well. Tragic. The whole thing is quite tragic."

"Indeed. Odd that she could in fact be so heavily involved in Seattle's seedy underbelly to the extent that it cost her her life and yet still put in seventy-hour work weeks here while passing each and every drug test Silverman-Chase had her take. Very curious to say the least."

"Well, she was a very resourceful woman. And I'm not sure I like your tone, Mister Butler." According to the narrator a 'veneer of civility' has completely vanished from our discussion. Okay.

"I'm sure you don't." I let the tension build some more with a multi-second pause. "What if I were to tell you that I've heard of a company out of Phoenix that…arranges for highly-paid-yet-unwanted executives with unfavorable contracts to be…let's say… 'taken care of' in a manner that makes them easily disposable to their employers? Have you ever heard of something like this being done?"

Chase doesn't say a word.

"We both know that Olivia was no cokehead and that she wasn't killed by drug dealers." Damn I'm awesome right now. "But if you stop bullshitting me and tell me what you DO know, I'll refrain from filling the police in on your little arrangement with Sancus, Inc."

We sit there silently staring at each other for a while, overwrought drama enveloping us like a cocoon. At some point Chase clears his throat and tells me plainly that he had absolutely nothing to do with Jennings' murder and that he hasn't been able to get in contact with Sancus since her body was discovered. He's on the verge of tears and is begging me to believe him so I do.

«««—»»»

The Rocky Mountains loom like some kind of mystical pantheon on the horizon as I approach the Mile High City. I'm racking my brain trying to figure out how the pieces of the Jennings murder all fit together. Since Silverman-Chase had nothing to do with it maybe Tetrace *was* solely responsible like The Wizard thought? What would that accomplish besides allowing Holbrook to freak me out back in the desert though? None of it is making any sense and I'm getting really goddamn frustrated and then some kind of electronic pulse surges through my head and I suddenly understand implicitly that Jennings' murder was completely unrelated to me or Holbrook or any of this shit. She was killed by some shady clients whose money she fucked with. That's it. The timing was just a coincidence and Chase was indeed telling me the truth.

I feel giddy as the electro-pulse sensation that somehow wired the information directly into my brain dissipates into a pleasurable numbness that resonates throughout my entire body.

THE SPARTAK TRIGGER

The narrator's embarrassed for some reason and then he starts talking about some fishing trip he went on once, bitching about a red herring that got away from him. I yell at him to shut the hell up and then I pull over to the side of the road and scream gibberish at the top of my lungs.

«‹‹—›»»

It turns out that Daniels is dead after all which is good I guess since it means I don't have to go marching into the lion's den at Tetrace HQ. Apparently The Wizard couldn't find his obituary because his birth name was something weird (Polish-sounding) and that's the handle they used in the paper and on the tombstone. I visit Daniels' grave and there's some woman there who I guess must be the widow. She asks me how I knew the deceased and I tell her we were gay lovers.

«‹‹—›»»

On my way back to Phoenix I pick up a hitchhiker in New Mexico. He tells me his name's Rolf and that he's a psychology major at some school I've never heard of. There's something about the kid that's inherently contradictory. I can't quite put my finger on it. His voice holds a quality that seems almost otherworldly and his conversation skills oscillate between sophisticated and juvenile at a supersonic rate.

We talk about politics and shit and he says he worked on the president's campaign team which I suppose is pretty impressive. The narrator's voice begins to tremble when he describes Rolf's handsome facial features and bizarrely-retro hair style. I ask the kid what he knows about Tetrace and he says he's never heard of it. I tell him it's the biggest website on the internet and then he asks me what the internet is.

«««—»»»

After our 'desultory' conversation hits a dead end Rolf and I somehow decide that we should visit a brothel. I try to call Roger on my cell phone to get him to hook us up with reservations somewhere but I can't get service.

We pull into a gas station in Santa Fe and the clerk eagerly tells us about an upscale whorehouse in Rio Rancho that sounds pretty awesome. It takes us about an hour to drive to the place and when we get there they demand a thousand dollars in cash before they let us in the front door. I hand the money over to the fat bastard guarding the entrance and he has to count it four times even though it's in hundreds. Idiot.

«««—»»»

I climb off of the mulatto-looking slut who made me wear two rubbers and get dressed pretty quickly. She asks me if I'm satisfied and I tell her she should work on her fake-orgasm-acting and she thanks me for the constructive feedback with a disgusting amount of genuineness. I walk downstairs and ask where Rolf is and they tell me he disappeared. They have no idea what happened to him. Whatever.

Just as I'm getting ready to leave another John walks in the door. I study his face for a moment and then I realize that he's Jester—a fellow Sancus agent.

«««—»»»

Jester shakes my hand uneasily and tells me his real name is Devin Smith. Way off-sides protocol-wise but I suppose under the circumstances it'll be okay. I give him my real name too. Jester asks the Madame if the two of us can borrow one of her rooms to talk for a bit and she says he'll have to pay their full rate and he tells her to throw it on his tab.

THE SPARTAK TRIGGER

We ascend a pretty cool baronial staircase and make our way into a small room on the second floor. Jester grabs a seat at the foot of an unmade bed while I lean against an antique dresser. My former co-worker lights a cigar with an extra-long match and takes a deep puff. "Pretty funny running into you here, Maverick."

"Yeah. Funny."

"You still living in Phoenix?" he asks, apparently oblivious to my fugitive status.

"Sort of. I've kind of been jumping around since the fire."

"What fire?" Jester casually blows a smoke ring exactly like Holbrook did back in San Jose. He's looking at me with a severe nonchalance that doesn't seem possible. I ask him if he's been out of the country or something and he tells me he just got back from a trip to South Africa. I explain to him that an arsonist burned our head office to the ground a few weeks ago. "Dave and Shelly both bought it," I say, gravely.

Jester stands up and looks at me like I'm crazy. "I just saw Dave and Shelly yesterday." He takes another puff of the cigar. "At the Sancus office in Scottsdale."

«‹‹—›»»

Every single radio station on the dial is re-broadcasting an old recording of Orson Welles' *War of the Worlds* for some reason so I turn the volume all the way down and begin to reprimand the narrator for forcing me to endure such a convoluted and nonsensical sequence of events.

"This plot makes is ridiculous!" I scream, putting the car in cruise control. "Plus the constant genre-splicing comes across as being hackneyed and lazy, there's no way this can work!"

The narrator just chuckles to himself then tells me to shut up and enjoy the ride prior to launching into an incredibly boring and melodramatic description of the 'lavishly barren' and 'desolately scenic' landscape I'm driving through at the moment. Weirdo.

«««—»»»

The Wizard looks even sicklier than the last time I'd seen him but when I ask him how he's doing he says that he's never felt better. Then he starts going on about his stupid neo-Bolshevik computer hacker conspiracy theory again so I tell him to zip it.

After giving him shit for sending me on a wild goose chase, I tell The Wizard that I'm fed up with playing Holbrook's game and that I'm not going to bother completing the last mission. He's pissed off and says that he can't get into PokerSphere's mainframe through any conventional hacking methods which means that Tetrace is for sure going to wipe out his hard drive. I tell him that I don't give a damn then I leave and get drunk at the first bar I come across.

«««—»»»

I've been wandering around the city for several hours. I spot an unfamiliar, fancy-looking art gallery at an upcoming intersection. It's called The Stroupe. I decide to take a look inside, just to take my mind off of things.

An exhibit called *Calypso Martyrdom* is being featured on the gallery's main floor. There are dozens of patrons crowded around a large glass case in the central showroom. I negotiate my way inside.

All I can see in the case is completely naked, badly-wounded man holding a scalpel in his right hand. Blood is smeared all along the interior of his transparent enclosure and when I move closer I see what appear to be large chunks of human flesh littered throughout the display.

"How long has he been at this?" I hear someone ask in the fingernails-on-chalkboard voice of a two-pack-a-day smoker.

"Couple hours," his buddy replies. "He's running out of non-vital organs though. He should be done soon."

I start to feel nauseous and walk away, into a high-ceilinged hall filled with classical-looking sculptures. I only take the time to look at one: a life-sized self-portrait-by-artist in granite, the exposed left arm apparently made of flesh, bone, skin, and cartilage. The queasy feeling intensifies.

The narrator joyously refers to the gallery's patrons as being "intellectual and cultural elitists" as he's forced to shout above the increasingly-loud combination of inane chatter and an out-of-tune piano. Then I hear someone, a woman I think, claim that this exhibition is "Ground Zero for Masochistic Expressionism" as I enter yet another showroom.

The first thing I see in this one is a large canvas smeared with dried blood. A video recording is playing on a continuous loop next to it: an Auschwitz-thin albino is sitting on a stool in front of a blank canvas the same size and make as what's currently on display before me. After staring into the camera for a few seconds he takes out a revolver. Then he puts it in his mouth and the screen goes black. A loud gunshot rings out and then the skeleton-man is back sitting on the stool as the video restarts.

I put my head down and quickly make my way out of the gallery. The narrator is ridiculing me mercilessly as I stumble awkwardly into a dense urban wasteland. A foreign cabbie yells something at me in his coarse native language as he drives by. I choose to ignore him, increasing my walking speed threefold, guided by a sense of urgency I'm not sure anyone's ever felt before in the history of humanity. And the narrator agrees. Wholeheartedly.

《《《—》》》

I tell Roger that I need to make some money before I take off for Mexico and he says it's my lucky day because he's hiring at the moment.

"What's the job?" I wipe some powdery residue from the edge of my subnasal passage.

"I'm putting a crew together. We're going down to the border and taking these Guido assholes out once and for all, show them they can't push us around in our own backyard. How does twenty grand sound?"

"Thirty sounds better."

"Done."

<<<—>>>

There are six of us in the van. Roger's driving and he's coked out of his mind as we travel down the interstate going about double the posted speed limit. I tell him he should slow down but he just laughs and tells me that the state troopers around here are easier to pay off than the relatives of deceased Middle Eastern prostitutes. Interesting simile. Or maybe it's a metaphor. Either way.

The other guys Roger's hired for this job are a lot younger than me. A couple of them look like they're straight out of high school. I ask the youngest-looking one if he's ever fired a gun before and he just looks at me with blank eyes and explains in graphic detail how he's taken part in a dozen drive-by-shootings this month alone. His friends all laugh and then they start talking about some slut they've all banged and I learn of the phrase "Eskimo brothers" for the first time.

"Grade-A crew you've got here, Rog," I proclaim.

My ex-partner snaps and tells me to mind my fucking business. It's best to leave him alone when he gets like this so I just ignore him and open up the newspaper I've brought with me to kill time on the drive. The cover story is about that guy from TV with the lazy eye who paid people cash for their old gold and electronics—apparently he was doing that as part of some massive illegal money laundering and smuggling operation designed to circumvent all kinds of international trade laws. He just got busted for it yesterday and in the story's main photo he's giving reporters the finger as he's being led to jail which I guess is pretty badass.

The secondary story is about a bunch of college kids in some online club called the Mayhem Society that had federal charges pressed against them after causing mass panic in a bunch of cities by reporting fake terrorist attacks over Chirrup in some kind of super-coordinated manner. I guess that's a pretty funny prank. The narrator starts talking about how virtual reality IS reality but I guess he doesn't have any meat to his argument so he kind of just trails off, embarrassed.

A somewhat related article in the main section is about a serial killer who was caught in Texas a few days ago after slaughtering dozens of women throughout the southwest. Apparently he'd been live-Chirping the entire murder spree but police thought it was phony for some reason and now they look like idiots after so many people died. The psycho looks exactly like that Rolf kid I picked up hitchhiking back when I was in that other dimension or navigating a space/time temporal anomaly or whatever but it says this psycho's name is Chris Hagan so maybe it's him and maybe it's not. But it probably (definitely) is.

I read an article in the Cosmopolitan Section about a family from Maricopa County who's filed a lawsuit against some company in California that puts people in comas for months at a time so they can lose weight by living off of stored body fat. It's a class action suit that was initiated by the husband and siblings of an obese woman who'd signed up to be knocked out for four whole years. The company's lawyers claim that the woman voluntarily signed up to follow their medical team's recommendation and that the family doesn't have a case.

The family's spokesman, meanwhile, claims that the company just wanted to get as much money as possible from the woman (it apparently costs $10,000/month to be placed in a weight loss coma), and that the whole thing's just a massive scam. I suddenly have an idea to start a weight loss clinic that uses heroin to get clients skinny but then I remember that someone's already thought of that.

   Another article in the same section is about a punk band called Myopic Deity Convention that recently held a charity concert raising money to send over to the Chinese government to help them keep Tibet under their tyrannical reign. The lead singer says in his interview that they did it as a big F YOU to the phony corporate rock singers who lend their celebrity to fashionable causes like trying to "Free" Tibet. A large group of protesters showed up and there was apparently a violent melee at the club where the show was taking place. The guy who wrote the article seems to take great pleasure in recounting the irony of the Asian monk-loving pacifists' vicious actions towards M.D.C. as they took the stage—brick throwing, equipment trashing, etc.

At the end of the article the writer mentions that another local band that plays something called thrash-core is planning on holding a concert to raise money to send to North Korea for them to spend on developing weapons of mass destruction. The band, which is called Sudden Infant Death Syndrome, has dubbed its upcoming show THE CONCERT TO NUKE AMERICA. Cool.

After glancing at the sports page and the comics for a bit I read an article in the Business Section about a new product our friends at MetroTech are unveiling in the next few days that will apparently revolutionize the personal mobile communications industry. This thing is called a "zComm" and is surgically implanted in the user's cerebral cortex. It can store a thousand gigabytes worth of music and user-friendly applications in addition to acting as a hands-free smartphone that can somehow interacts with your brain waves. The zComm apparently just needs for you to think of someone and it dials their number and shit. Pretty crazy.

MetroTech's CEO is quoted several times making grandiose claims about the ground-breaking hands-free device, which will retail for $999.99 with a medical procedural fee of $149.50 built in. An extended warranty is available, as is a generous life insurance policy in case of accidental death during installation or use. Nice touch.

<<<—>>>

The National Defense Militia's main compound is located about an hour south of Tucson but we get there in forty minutes

THE SPARTAK TRIGGER

after gassing up near U of A's main campus and nearly running over some loser who's trying to drum up business for a car wash by spinning a huge cardboard sign around and pestering disinterested travellers. Roger's got the campaign planned out pretty well and he splits us up into teams of two. He's got a map of the place somehow and the main entrances/exits are divvied up as we all take our AK-47 rifles and hand grenades. The narrator's voice lowers an octave as he gaily describes the 'overt machismo' oozing out of all of us as we stealthily take our positions and prepare to partake in a gunfight with gangsters posing as delusional patriots.

《《《—》》》

Roger's sweating profusely and when I ask him if he's okay he tells me to fuck off in a three-pronged whiplash of a whisper. I suddenly realize that my ex-partner might be suicidal and looking to go out in a blaze of glory but I don't have time to deliberate this point because it's 3:39 A.M. and we're meant to execute our coordinated strike in less than a minute.

"You ready for this, dude?" Roger asks me in his normal speaking voice. I nod formally and stroke the barrel of my machine gun sensually. *Rock 'n' Roll.*

There's an awkward pause in the action and then the editor starts giving the narrator crap about the alarming number of typos and other such gaffes that he's finding in this allegedly "finished" manuscript. The narrator defends himself by claiming that he's *intentionally* included a specific quantity of typos various other grammatical/syntax-related mistakes in order to give his work an 'unstructured, spontaneous, Kerouac-esque' feel.

Some marketing exec chimes in and starts blathering on about a half-baked promotional idea involving a contest whereby readers who find every mistake in THE SPARTAK TRIGGER win a prize or something but then the narrator seems to get annoyed with the guy and admits the whole 'intentional typo' thing was just a way to cover up his sloppy writing and extreme laziness. Groovy.

We burst through the compound's back door right at 3:40 and the night vision goggles we're wearing seem to work okay. It takes us a few seconds to find the bunk area and the other teams show up at exactly the same time as us. We line up in a row and Roger counts down from five on his right hand. When he runs out of digits and makes a fist each of us empties a clip into the sleeping members of the N.D.M. and only one or two of them wake up long enough to see a bunch of shadowy figures taking their lives from them. No one seems to notice that I shot straight into a wall which I guess doesn't even matter since Roger's getting what he paid for regardless if I actually kill anyone or not. I'm here. That's all that matters.

The whole thing is over in less than fifteen seconds and a 'profound hush' falls over the room as we all start looking at each other curiously. "That's that," Roger murmurs. "Good job, boys. Kinda surprised they didn't have someone standing guard, but whatever."

We walk out of the compound and get back in the van. We drive back to Phoenix. Mission accomplished.

Roger hands me my thirty grand in a used personal-sized pizza box and wishes me luck in Mexico. For some reason we start talking about how it's too bad we can't retcon the canon of our personal histories which is pretty weird I guess. I shake his hand and examine his hardened face for one last time. His eyes are dead but not entirely lifeless; it's as if they've just been violently prodded from an eternal slumber by some kind of zombie voodoo sex ritual. The narrator says he's grinning 'lasciviously' and grasping my hand in a 'vicelike' grip which is the half-truth at best.

"I guess I'll see you in Hell, partner," Roger says, suddenly realizing that I'm leaving the country forever. His words are left hanging there, suspended in midair by some kind of supernatural forces field.

THE SPARTAK TRIGGER

《《《——》》》

I walk out of Roger's office and Holbrook's Australian thug grabs me by my free arm. He throws me against the building and works me over for a bit, mostly hammering my solar plexus with his canned-ham-sized fists. He lets up for a few seconds and I keel over and throw up my breakfast which is mostly undigested chunks of fast food.

"You should really start eating healthier, Bishop," Frederick tells me. A muffled "fuck you" is the best I can offer as a response. He picks me up off the ground and leads me over to a jet-black luxury car. I try to fight him off but he's way too strong. He laughs at my efforts and I suddenly think I might start to cry.

Holbrook's sitting cross-legged in the back of his stretched limo and a nice-looking tuxedo's clinging to what the narrator refers to as a 'graceful build.' "Nice to see you again, Bishop." Holbrook pretends to take a sip from an empty martini glass.

I tell Holbrook he can go fuck himself and he cackles hysterically as he motions for his Aussie goon to leave us alone. The hulking foreigner tosses my pizza box at me and slams the car door shut, leaving Holbrook and I alone in the spacious rear cabin.

"So," Holbrook says playfully. "I understand you've decided to renege upon our little agreement, yes?"

I don't say anything and then Holbrook tosses a legal-sized envelope at me. "Take a look at those."

My hands are shaking as I break the seal on the envelope and remove a set of glossy 8x10 photos. The naked, bloodied corpse of The Wizard is depicted in every shot and I'm gasping for air as an invisible dagger stabs me in the windpipe.

"As I understand it your latest identity has yet to be compromised, correct?" Holbrook's face has contorted into a mask of 'savage triumph.'

I nod after a moment and Holbrook claps his hands excitedly as his martini glass falls to the floor. "Excellent!" he yelps. "That means you're more than capable of completing the final phase of your mission. Only one more site to take down if I'm not mistaken—an alarmingly-popular gambling URL which is run by a corrupt tribe of Indians up north. This should be a snap to execute for a clever lad such as yourself."

Holbrook tosses a pear-shaped flash disc into my lap and tells me that my flight to Albany leaves in an hour. He confidently makes his way out of the limo, which springs to life and starts to drive off as soon as he slams the door shut behind him. I watch myself begin to weep and the narrator calls me a pussy in an uncharacteristically-pithy fashion. I tell him to leave me the hell alone and he snickers arrogantly before making some snide comments and comparing the tears rolling down my reddened face to dew descending along the side of a ripened tomato.

«««—»»»

My northeastward flight has a lengthy layover in St. Louis and I spend a half-hour playing pinball at the airport arcade. Some snot-nosed little kid challenges me to a race on some virtual video car driving game and I kick his ass then taunt him mercilessly until he runs away sobbing. The kid's mother comes and finds me to give me an earful but as soon as I tell her she should think about getting Botox she gets so flustered that she can't even form proper sentences.

«««—»»»

The snowstorm I'm driving through is pretty intense. I'm only going 20 miles an hour and, as far as I can tell, mine is the only car on the highway. The narrator tries to give me some tips on driving in severe weather but I outright ignore him and turn the classic metal station I've been listening to up full blast as I spot a sign on the side of the road that tells me I'm only four miles away from the St. Regis Mohawk Reservation. After a couple of anthemic choruses I turn the station down and catch the narrator flagrantly breaking whatever number wall we're at now and whispering a bunch of stuff to you that I guess he doesn't want me to hear. Whatever.

I see a 'blurred nebula' of flashing red and white lights in the distance and before I figure out what's going on I'm right on top of a pair of squad cars stopped in the middle of the road. I slam on the breaks but the icy road propels me forward into the back of one of them. I shout out a series of non-sequiturs as I climb out of my cheap rental car and a powerful wind knocks me to the ground.

Angry and sore, I stand up and slowly make my way over to the front of the police vehicle I rear-ended. When I look inside the passenger window I see two cops sitting perfectly still. Their eyes are closed and dried blood is caking each of their chins. I finally notice that their windshield's been festooned with several bullet holes and I check both cops' pulses for some reason even though they're both obviously dead. Steam is billowing from their still-fresh wounds so now I'm paninervous (sic) on top of everything else. Great.

I check the other car and one of the cops is still alive. He's covered in blood too and his partner is hunched over against the steering wheel, his brains spilled out onto the dashboard. I almost puke from the sight and stench of the guy. The barely-living officer begs me to help him in a whimper that's barely audible beneath the deafening howl of the raging storm enveloping us.

"What's your name, buddy?" I shout.

"Sergeant…Dwayne…Simpson."

I tell Dwayne not to move and I quickly inspect the damage he's sustained. He doesn't appear to be shot in any vital areas but when I give him the good news he just coughs and curses out the group of renegade Indian terrorists that apparently ambushed them as some kind of protest against White American authority figures.

Before I'm able to reach over and grab their radio to call for an ambulance a fucking arrow hits me in the leg and an overture of gunshots thunders through the icy silence, tearing into

Dwayne's throat as well as the hood of his squad car. One of the bullets grazes my arm and I scramble for cover as the unseen attackers unleash a series of terrifyingly battle cries. Another round of gunfire goes off and then I'm covered in broken glass as both squad cars' rear windows shatter in slow motion. I hear myself issue a cowardly yelp as I fall to the frozen asphalt.

I'm staring up into the dense white sky as I notice a throbbing pain burrowing into my stomach. I look up and see another arrow sticking up out of my gut and I shake my head in disapproval as a 'rapacious fury' courses through me. I try to pull the arrow out but my strength seems to have left me and the back of my head hits the cold ground as everything begins to fade into a glorious blur which in turn dissolves into a blackness that can only be described as 'absolute.'

«««—»»»

I open my eyes and after a few seconds I realize that I'm in a hospital bed. There are all kinds of tubes and wires and shit running out of me and I'm hooked into some machine that's bleeping every two seconds or so.

An elderly, avuncular physician is standing over me soon enough. He tells me that I'm lucky to be alive so hooray for me. The doctor takes out a clipboard and lists off all of the injuries I've sustained and what they've done to fix me and whatnot. His voice sounds an awful lot like the narrator's.

The doc tells me to get some rest and he leaves the room. I stare up at the ceiling and think about that stupid fumble I made back in college. The scene's remarkably vivid in my mind—I catch the ball near the sidelines, break a tackle then the thing just slips out of my hands and a rival free safety recovers it and runs straight into our end zone. Maybe if I'd just held on to that ball everything would've turned out differently for me. Probably not though. I still would've found a way to fuck things up.

THE SPARTAK TRIGGER

《《《—》》》

The flat-panel TV my hospital room comes with doesn't have a remote control and the channel's set to a 24/7 news station that keeps showing live footage of the standoff between New York state troopers and dissident residents of the St. Regis Indian Reservation. Apparently the RCMP is doing the same thing on the Canadian side. The news people aren't sure what instigated the natives' violent attacks but they bring in some anthropologist who postulates a series of preposterous theories that I guess I don't really understand.

《《《—》》》

I realize I'll have to answer questions from the authorities at some point so I start to think of possible explanations as to why I'm in upstate New York in the middle of winter. It takes me a while just to remember my latest fake name and then I figure that they'll probably discover my real identity pretty easily once they start digging and then I'll definitely be sent back to San Diego to stand trial for the Zimmerman murder. So that would suck.

Just as I'm struggling to get to my feet the door to my room springs open and some short dweeb in a fancy overcoat and an old-fashioned bowler hat walks in. Without saying a word he 'saunters' over to the foot of my bed. The tiny, well-dressed stranger looks down at me with a mischievous gleam in his beady little eyes. "Looks like you've had a rough week, eh Bishop?"

"Who the hell are you?" I demand.

The bastard tells me that while I wasn't able to make it to PokerSphere's headquarters to upload Tetrace's virus onto their mainframe, the lengthy standoff between the reserve's heavily-armed inhabitants and authorities on both sides of the border has managed to disrupt the website's affairs to the point where it's no longer operable anyway.

"Well that's just swell." I'm seething, speaking through

harshly-ground teeth. "Now. Answer my fucking question. Who the hell are you?"

"My name is Tristan Miller." My visitor reaches out to shake my hand and I reluctantly oblige the custom, my brain once again going into hyper-confusion mode. "I work for Metro Technologies Limited, colloquially known as MetroTech." Interesting.

"What are you doing here?" I ask.

Miller grabs a plastic chair and places it next to my bed. He sits down, crosses his legs and folds his hands atop his lap. "We've been watching you for quite some time now, Bishop."

"Is that so?"

"It is actually. We pay close attention to those in the employ of our biggest competitors, especially those whose job descriptions involve corporate espionage or…sabotage." Miller's expression has shifted from warm and relaxed to cold and calculating.

"Tetrace." I can't help my tone from sounding indignant.

"Precisely. As you know, our two companies have been battling for quite some time."

"Right, over who's got the biggest slice of the internet pie."

A smug look overtakes Miller's shriveled face and he once again alters his temperament, as if it's as easy as flicking a switch. "Shane, Shane, Shane. You disappoint me. You think in such small terms. What we're really battling over is control…of the world."

I try to recall the details of The Wizard's semi-coherent ramblings about the conspiracy he was working on unraveling before Holbrook took him out but I can't. Something about the former Soviet Union I think. And social media. A code of some kind. The narrator won't help me remember any specific details, claiming that he's not a fan of something called 'internal analepsis.' Asshole. Then he apologizes in advance for all of the impending exposition but promises some more action soon as well so that'll be good.

I stare forcefully into my visitor's stern, stolid face. "What does all of this have to do with me? And what's it got to do with the Russians?" Miller seems somewhat taken aback by the second part of my question.

THE SPARTAK TRIGGER

"Well. Perhaps I've underestimated you. Maverick." Miller's brittle voice alters in mid-sentence from a playful twang to something far more sinister. "Tell you what. Since you've managed to beat the odds and stay alive this long I'll fill you in on more details than I've been authorized to provide. Sound good?"

"Such generosity." The narrator begins to chime in about something completely unrelated so I tell him aloud to pipe down but Miller doesn't seem to notice. He unfolds his legs and leans forward in his chair as he begins to explain to me what the fuck is going on with this meandering, convoluted plot you've managed to tolerate thus far.

"Several months ago—right as we were getting ready to launch Bleep dot com—one of our moles in Tetrace's Competitive Intelligence Department alerted us that they would be making an unprecedented move to disrupt every single one of their chief competitors' operations in one fell swoop. We knew this would come very quickly after they outbid us in the ChumSpot auction, a prize we planned on losing all along yet drew out for as long as it took us to develop a strategic counter-attack to their forthcoming offensive."

Miller pauses and looks at me like he's worried about me not paying attention or something. He continues his story after a few seconds of mutual discomfort.

"So. Since Tetrace knew full well that we had all of their covert operatives under surveillance, they obviously had to entice someone outside of their organization to complete their ambitious gambit. They rightly assumed we'd be monitoring the activities of any and all known freelance digital security terrorists, meaning they had to use someone off the grid, someone we wouldn't suspect."

"Namely. Me." The narrator claims I'm 'disconsolate' but I feel completely fine, believe me.

"Precisely." Miller's gaze intensifies into a penetrating glare. "This was a move our tactical computer system managed to predict, however. Given than Sancus was the only company in the U.S. that performed such…unique services for its customers, we were able to anticipate that Tetrace would indeed hire your firm and proceed to manipulate an elaborate series of events so as to attain their goal of web dominance. With your background being what it is and with your established ties to the Arizona underworld, it was obvious that you would be the agent they would ultimately target upon placing Sancus on a retainer."

"Flattering."

"Indeed. At any rate, we remained one step ahead of Tetrace the entire time they were planning and executing this foolhardy plot of theirs. Did you not find it odd that you were able to infiltrate our corporate headquarters and implant a virus on our system with such ease?" I don't answer him. I don't have to.

"That website we allowed you to take down was merely an exercise in misdirection." Miller's smirking exultantly. "Launching Bleep as a direct opponent of Tetrace's flagship enterprise was a futile endeavor, we knew that. But it distracted them long enough to allow us to proceed with Operation Nero without interruption."

"What the fuck is 'Operation Nero?'"

"Something we've been working on for quite some time. I noticed on your transcript from ASU that you in fact failed a survey course on ancient history so I'll assume you aren't familiar with the Roman Emperor Nero?"

Nope. "Nope. I do remember that class though. The professor was a real asshole."

Miller's head snaps sideways a split second before the door to my room again swings open. By the time Holbrook and Frederick spot Miller and reach for their guns he's already done a frontwards somersault and hurled a throwing knife through each of their throats. Both men issue bone-chilling gurgling sounds and fall to the ground in perfect unison, as if they'd rehearsed a synchronized death routine. "Speaking of assholes," Miller quips.

Without hesitation Miller retrieves his knives from his victims' necks, wipes the blood off of them with a monogramed handkerchief and places them back into his overcoat. He then disappears back into the hospital corridor and when he returns a few minutes later he's got a couple of gurneys with him. I ask him where he got them and he says the morgue. His overcoat and hat are both gone and now he's wearing the bright turquoise uniform of a medical orderly.

Miller starts whistling the theme song to a popular prime time teen soap opera as he swiftly manages to strip Holbrook and the Aussie down to their underwear and toss their lifeless corpses onto the stolen gurneys. He's amazingly strong for such a small guy. "Need a hand?" I ask. "Nope, all good," Miller replies, casually. He cauterizes the still-bleeding wounds of Holbrook and Frederick—who he refers to as 'dirty Tetrites'—with a pocket lighter and furiously fills out a pair of toe tags that he attaches to his deceased enemies' feet.

"I'll be back in a minute," Miller proclaims before dragging both wheeled benches back into the hallway. As soon as he's gone I leap out of bed to make my escape but a sudden, excruciating headache forces me back into bed where I writhe in agony for what feels like forever.

The blindingly intense pain stops as soon as Miller reappears. He sits back down in the exact same pose he'd made use of earlier.

"Now, where were we?" he asks.

"Emperor Nero." A single strand of blood is dripping down my chin. I wipe it away with the back of my right hand.

"Right. Well, when Nero ascended to the throne in fifty-four A.D. he was most displeased with Rome from a variety of standpoints. Ten years later, still not satisfied with his city, he burnt it to the ground so he could rebuild it as he saw fit. And while Rome burned he played the fucking fiddle. How cool is that? This is exactly what we mean to do. We will destroy the World…Wide Web…and remake it in our image."

The poignancy and depth in Miller's voice is nothing short of resolute. It seems crazy but he's entirely serious about all of this.

"That's impossible," I tell him. "It's too big. You can't just erase the internet. Even I know that."

"That's where you're wrong. There's a mechanism already in place to do exactly that. I'm afraid properly explaining it will require another history lesson though if that's alright."

"Sure, why not?"

"You were born in the early-sixties so you're just a little too young to remember the impact felt in this country when the Soviets launched Sputnik in nineteen fifty-seven. I'm sure you've heard of the program though, yes? In school and such?" I nod.

Exuding the 'obstinate bravado' of a cartoon super villain, Miller goes on to explain that the U.S. government created the Advanced Research Projects Agency as a response to Sputnik's success and the enhanced threat of a nuclear attack that accompanied the satellite's orbiting of the planet. "The A.R.P.A.'s first assignment was to develop a nationwide communications system which would enhance the military's ability to ensure that America could respond to any external attack with lightning-fast rapidity. What they ultimately developed was the world's first operational packet switching network, a hierarchical routing configuration which utilized a series of Interface Message Processors, or 'I.M.P.s.' They called it the 'ARPANET' at the time. It eventually evolved into what we now know as the 'internet,' a global system of interconnected networks whose foundation remains rooted in the inter-I.M.P. circuitry developed by the A.R.P.A. back in the sixties."

"Fascinating."

"Here's the good part." Miller stands up and gently places his palms atop the side of my bed. "What almost no one on Earth realizes, including every significant branch of the United States' intelligence community, is that one of the principle engineers working on the ARPANET project was in actuality a Soviet spy named Vladimir Kozlov, aka Walter Sherman—codename 'Spartak.' The K.G.B. directed him to secretly embed an override command function deep within the programming language he was working on, a trigger which could immediately shut the whole thing down. You might say it was the original piece of spyware."

I don't get the joke Miller just made and he looks like he might explain it to me since he clearly thinks it was clever but then he lets it go and continues with his speech. "Anyway, the idea was that if the Russians launched a preemptive nuclear attack on us, they could totally black out our military's communications before they made their move, making the whole continent of North America one big sitting duck."

To be honest I don't follow everything Miller's telling me but I think I get what he's saying overall. "How do you know all of this?"

"Let's just say the information didn't come cheap. At any rate, Spartak successfully faked his own death and smuggled his network cessation algorithm and its trigger sequence back to Russia on a microfilm. The Soviets stored it in a top secret facility outside of Stalingrad. Luckily, they never did attack the U.S. with nuclear weapons, meaning the data was kept on lockdown until the U.S.S.R. ultimately collapsed."

"What is this trigger then? A virus or something?"

"Not exactly—we've been told that it's a simple twelve-digit keyboard sequence that, when punched-in under the correct settings, instigates an immediate system-wide shutdown. It'd be like hitting ALT-CONTROL-DELETE on your P.C."

"Wait—so *anyone* could accidentally hit a bunch of random keys on their computer in a certain order and accidentally shut the whole internet down?"

"No. For the trigger to work you need to be synced in with the original data platform Spartak wrote the sequence on. You'd have to be hooked into an old-fashioned transistor computer and rig it up to be able to get onto the modern incarnation of the internet. It wouldn't be too difficult for a decent computer engineer to pull off…if he had the microfilm containing the Spartak Trigger that is."

I finally realize where all this is going. "And I suppose you have an idea where this microfilm is at present?"

Miller slowly shuffles over to a window on the far side of the room. He takes a deep breath. "Near the end of the Cold War a high-ranking member of the Russian military—a hardline communist—retrieved the Spartak Trigger right before their government collapsed completely. From there it somehow ended up in the hands of underground social agitators still loyal to the Marxist cause. They fancy themselves 'anarchists' but we'd call them 'terrorists' in this country. We believe this group is planning on using the trigger in the very near future, to throw the world into a state of unrest from which they believe socialism will emerge as the dominant political philosophy. The internet crashing completely would indeed cripple the global financial market, which has become wholly dependent upon online commerce. I don't need to tell you that results of this happening would indeed be catastrophic. The threat these anarchists pose is great to say the least."

Miller coolly snaps his fingers and smiles at me with perverse satisfaction. "Wait a minute," I say, buoyantly. "Are these anarchist guys communicating with each other over Chirrup via some bullshit code-talk by any chance?"

"As a matter of fact we believe that they are. How did you know that?"

"Just a hunch. So, basically, MetroTech is scrambling to snag this microfilm before the terrorists can use it?"

"Exactly. Our programmers have already developed a new network to take the place of the World Wide Web. Every single website on the internet will cease to exist and from the ashes of this destruction, the MetroNet will rise—like a Phoenix from the flames. We just need to launch it at the *exact* instant the Spartak Trigger is activated for the plan to work. Even a second's delay would make the entire endeavor futile." Miller pauses to make sure I'm impressed. I guess I am. "If…*once* we succeed, MetroTech will have one hundred percent ownership of the internet. Operation Nero will deliver us to a level of prominence never before seen in human civilization—every bit of information on the planet's most powerful communication tool will be controlled by us. All we need is a fifty-year-old microfilm to make it happen."

THE SPARTAK TRIGGER

The narrator suddenly sounds frightened. His voice quivers ever-so-slightly as he describes Miller's demeanor at the moment, which he actually does a pretty decent job of.

"So I'm guessing you want me to help out with the hunt for this elusive microfilm," I say. "That's why you're here isn't it? That's why you're regaling me with all of these farfetched tales?"

"You are correct." Miller releases a heavy sigh. "Our efforts to track down and infiltrate the group in question have thus far proven…unsuccessful. Too many of our agents are well-known within the European espionage community, corporate and otherwise. As time is of the essence, we felt that it would be in our best interest to try something new—namely sending an unknown agent into the field who's shown tremendous promise both as a detective and as a covert proxy. Someone we've already invested a great deal of time and money into yet is also expendable."

"Thanks."

Miller takes a pair of envelopes out of his inside coat pocket. "So. As soon as you've healed up here you'll be on the first plane to Russia." He lays the envelopes on my nightstand. "The papers for your new identity are all here along with a limitless international credit card and a few thousand Euros to get you started. One of our operatives will meet you at the airport in Moscow and bring you up to speed on his findings. In the event that you're indeed able to retrieve the Spartak Trigger, you will be rewarded to the tune of two million dollars. Do we have an understanding?"

It's déjà vu all over again.

He's serious. He's actually serious. "What the fuck?" I cry out, incredulously. "Why the hell would I want to help you assholes out with this shit? I've already been through enough, don't you think? Plus I don't even speak Russian, this is insane!"

Miller doesn't say anything but produces a small electronic device seemingly out of thin air. It's smaller than a cell phone but not by much. He pushes a few buttons on the thing and the back of my head starts to tingle. Then the pulsing sensation I've experienced a few times during this ordeal surges through me, this time even more intense than before. After a moment it stops and I'm desperately panting, drenched in sweat. "What the hell was that?" I gasp.

"Now you speak Russian," Miller says, coyly.

"Huh? `tchyo za ga`lima?" I hear myself say. "Jesus…eto piz`dets."

I ask Miller how what he just did to me is possible. "You've probably heard of the zComm system MetroTech will be launching in the very near future?"

"Yeah," I say. "I actually read an article about that the other day."

"Well that technology is actually four or five years old. We have a far more advanced neuro-comm system that will be released to consumers when the time is right for the next phase of our campaign to be implemented."

"Wait, so you're telling me there's a more advanced version of that zComm thing linked up to my brain right now?!" The narrator snickers at the level of helplessness I'm feeling at the moment. Jerk.

"That's exactly what I'm telling you." Miller sneezes and waits for me to say "bless you" or something but I don't. "It's actually a prototype of the third generation zComm receiver, which is at least four years away from commercial use. By the time our subscribers upgrade to the model we've installed in you, we'll be able to manipulate every aspect of their lives without them knowing it. Sure, they'll be able to learn a language or become intimately familiar with a foreign city's streets in a manner of seconds, but we'll be able to get people to buy certain brands of products—cola, cars, electronics, anything. We'll even be able to have our customers vote a certain way in a given election, all without their knowing. These services will of course be available to any party willing to take advantage, for a rather exorbitant sum of course."

Wow. They'll rule the world. The whole fucking thing. "Why are you telling me all of this?"

"What difference does it make? Even if you survive this assignment no one is going to listen to a washed-up murderous cop with outlandish delusions of grandeur?"

"Good point."

"You're actually one of the first test subjects for this particular neuro-com system." Miller acts like this is a big accomplishment, something I should be proud of. "As such, you may have experienced a few side effects since we installed it last month. The system is still in the testing phase and, unfortunately, a few rather serious glitches persist."

I feel the back of my head and run my fingers along the subtle scar engraved within the base of my skull. "When... How the fuck did you install this thing in my head??" I feel like screaming and crying at the same time, as if I've been shackled in chains and dumped into a vat of liquid terror.

Miller tells me that they knew my modus operandi inside and out long before Tetrace hired Sancus. He says they'd followed me on several jobs and knew exactly how I executed every particular type of assignment. "Do you recall a mission Sancus sent you on out in Seattle?" I nod, gravely. Miller takes out his smartphone and fiddles with it for a few seconds before finding what he wants to show me. He holds the screen up for me to inspect. "Do you recognize this man?"

I take the phone and examine the photo he's retrieved from his files. "That's an amateur comedian I saw at a club once." A 'blanket of shock' asphyxiates me. "His stage name is Dickie Gunn."

"Right, Dickie Gunn. He's pretty good, isn't he?" Miller puts his zPhone away. "Hard to believe that was his first time on stage. His real name is Richard Gunderson. He's one of our best field agents. The cocaine you stole from him that night was laced with a rather potent anesthesia. We were quite certain that, given your history, you would indeed indulge in the tainted narcotics you stole in order to complete your frame-up assignment. While you were unconscious we broke into your motel room and performed the zComm installation procedure. Congratulations on that one by the way, getting whatshername arrested."

"Jennings. Her name was Jennings. Were you the ones who kill her?"

"No, we told you that already."

My dumfounded condition begins to abate and my senses all seem to be in good working order now. "What if I just refuse to help you? Even though two million bucks is two million bucks, the odds don't sound all that great that I'll make it out of this thing alive. So if I just say 'no,' what the hell can you do about it, short stack?"

Miller takes out the small device he'd used earlier to program my brain with Russian linguistic capabilities. He holds it high above his head and presses firmly upon a single button. The incredible pain I'd felt while Miller was disposing of the Tetrites' corpses returns and I'm quickly overtaken by a pain supernova, my fingers digging into the thin mattress I've been perched atop for the better part of a week. I try to scream but Miller quickly covers my mouth with his free mitt and issues a condescending '*shhhhh.*' As soon as he takes his hand away the pain stops.

Miller walks over to the door and looks back at me. I hang my head and tell him I'll get him the microfilm. "Good boy," he hisses as he disappears into the corridor. As soon as he's gone the narrator and I argue about whether we're at the end of the second act or beginning of the third. Either way it's a little late in the game to be introducing our eponymous MacGuffin but the narrator doesn't seem to care since he's not 'bound by the shackles of traditional storytelling.' Good for him.

«««—»»»

My flight to Moscow has a layover at JFK and there's a massive winter storm tormenting the northeast so the airline people tell me and thousands of other stranded passengers to "hang tight" for the time being. Awesome.

I buy a book called *Vegan in a Tiger Cage* and read it cover-to-cover. It's not as funny as it sounds.

I order a round of drinks for everyone at some novelty chain sports bar with MetroTech's credit card but no one even thanks me so I cancel the order and bolt.

THE SPARTAK TRIGGER

I eavesdrop on a pair of women—ugly, about my age—having a conversation about one of their teenaged sons' attempted suicide. I interrupt and ask if the kid's an organ donor. This blubbery bitch is taken aback and stammers that she's not sure as her skinny friend shoots me a fuckoff glare and tells me to mind my own business. I tell the fat one to make sure her kid fills out an organ donor card before he offs himself for real so that decent people can at least benefit and contribute to society in a meaningful manner. The friend yells for a security guard but there's none around and I just walk away.

A couple of nerds in their mid-thirties are creepily lurking about with a video camera and surreptitiously filming people who are walking while texting. I ask one of them what the hell they're doing and he tells me they're trying to catch someone walking into something funny on film—the wrong bathroom for their gender, an off-limits airport security area, a loaded baby carriage—while they're distracted by their smartphones.

"Like that woman at the mall who fell in the fountain?" I ask.

"Yeah," the guy tells me. "Only funnier! We've already got our own page on WatchThis dot com called Textalities—you should check it out some time, man."

"No chance. Good luck with your gay little video project, losers."

There's an old man wearing a Sun Devils jacket in the food court and I ask him if he wants an autograph. He studies my face for a minute and tells me to practice holding onto the ball better. "Fuck you, grandpa!" I shout at him as he's ordering a burrito.

The high-speed internet access kiosk is crowded with dorky Star Whatever-types and I think about The Wizard for a minute and feel a tiny bit of remorse but it soon passes. I linger around the area for a while and notice that most of them are playing around on Chirrup. I tap one of them on the shoulder and when he turns to face me I tell him to stop wasting his life. He asks me what I mean and I tell him that nobody gives a damn what he thinks about the Clone Wars or whatever. "Nobody gives a fuck what you think about anything." He thanks me for my advice and turns back to his laptop. The narrator goes on yet another lengthy rant about how blogs and shit make people feel important, as if their opinions matter somehow in the grand, ambivalent scheme of it all. Then he goes on and on about how social media sites like Chirrup give 'common folk' a fleeting, euphoric sense of relevance because they're superficially linked to the accounts of celebrities and famous athletes and shit. These 'flimsy, non-linear connections' somehow add meaning to peoples' lives he professes. I wait until he's finished the spiel before I abandon the dweeb-infested kiosk, wishing them luck living their lives 140 characters at a time.

One of the big airlines has a booth set up next to the only tavern in this terminal and they've got two broads stationed there trying to get people to sign up for some bullshit rewards program or something. I approach one of them and she blasts through eight sentences worth of hyperbole in ten seconds flat. Impressive. I tell her I'm not interested in the program and I'm pretty sure she gives me the exact same spiel again, doing her absolute best to keep me from interrupting while injecting a more desperate, pleading tone into her delivery.

When she's finally done I ask her how much commission she gets for adding new members to their program and she says she can't tell me. Bitch. Then the narrator goes off on yet another one of his tangents about how the whole concept of 'the sales process' has had an adverse effect on society as its essential function forces its practitioners to forge artificial relationships with people and that contrived disingenuousness ultimately permeates through all aspects of business and then life and the sense of phoniness the whole thing propagates somehow creates a gigantic society-wide menagerie forged upon false sentiments and blurred lines of motivations behind human interactions that even the salespeople themselves are confused by, even if they don't realize it. Whoa. Not sure I follow him on this one to be honest. Whatever, I'm thirsty.

I finish drinking a bottle of water and throw it into an open

THE SPARTAK TRIGGER

garbage bin. Some fucking hippy runs up to me and gives me hell for not recycling. "You're ruining the planet asshole!" He's in my face like a losing manager protesting a call to an umpire. I grab the moron by his dread locks and pull down until he's begging me to let him go and calling me a fascist.

"You're the fucking fascist, fucktard," I hiss into his ear. "You goddamn environmental activist types bully people into your way of thinking using scare tactics and shit, ridiculing anyone who doesn't want the world to be the way you want it to be. Let me tell you something kid, I know what the world's going to become and believe me—we're better off euthanizing the thing with pollution or whatever it is you waste your time protesting." I let him go and he runs away towards another terminal. The narrator says he's going to change his major at Woolcolmbe College from Eastern Philosophy to Business Administration next week. Cool.

«‹‹—›››

The girl next to me on the plane is a school teacher from Minnesota. Her name's Mulva or something. She's going to Moscow as part of some bullshit government exchange program that promotes cultural cohesion. I nod absently as she tells me all about her impending semester abroad and the stewardess keeps feeding me vodka tonics.

Mulva finally asks me why I'm going to Moscow. I tell her that I'm a covert double agent caught up in the middle of a 21st century Cold War involving a pair of rival technology-based corporations each hell-bent on world domination and that I need to retrieve a microfilm from a group of neo-commie anarchists before they use its contents to execute an instantaneous viral revolution that will obliterate modern society as we know it and send us back to the Analogue Age. She laughs and tells me I'm funny but then I send her an icy look that makes her pretty, young face morph into a trembling caricature of fear. Her mind is undoubtedly teeming with speculation as I get up to use the bathroom. When I return she's not there and I stretch my legs out gratefully as a 'feeling of tremendous pride' overtakes me… More or less anyway.

«««—»»»

When I finally arrive at Domodedovo International there's a balding boxer-looking dude waiting for me with a cardboard sign that has my latest alias—Sergei Markov—scrawled across it. The guy's wearing a pair of tattered blue jeans and a leather jacket and his pockmarked face is as hard and flat, like a frying pan. He introduces himself as Pavel Somethingorotherikov and pretty soon we're cruising around Moscow in his navy blue sedan.

"Where are we going?" I ask him after a while. I can't tell if I'm speaking Russian or English.

"To your hotel," Pavel replies. "You will spend the night here and tomorrow morning we will travel to Kazan."

"What's in Kazan?"

"A promising lead I have been pursuing for many weeks now." Pavel turns to face me with a 'surfeit of sternness' bursting out of his eyes. "Let me make something very clear to you, American. I did not ask for your help on this assignment. My superiors have insisted I bring you with me however. They pay me well so I will allow it. If you stay out of my way and do as I tell you there will be no problems between us, understand?"

"Sure."

Pavel slams on the brakes and I see we're at the hotel MetroTech booked for me so I grab my bag and get out. I slam the passenger door shut and my new partner puts a ski mask on. I ask him where he's going now and he tells me he's going to rape some girl he met on a Russian dating website.

"Good luck with that, man."

"Spasibo."

THE SPARTAK TRIGGER

《《《——》》》

I spend my first ever night in Europe exploring the city they taught us back in grade school was the epicenter of evil. The narrator goes overboard in describing the 'juxtaposing pageantry' of Moscow and doesn't even mention all of the smoking hot chicks I pass by on the sidewalk. Faggot.

Some fancy-pants businessman almost bumps into me on the sidewalk while he's reading something on his smartphone and I tell him to be more careful or he'll end up on Textalities and become a global laughing stock. He asks me what the hell I'm talking about and I turn and walk away.

A bunch of kids are photographing each other sitting in the middle of the street making a weird pose and the narrator explains that they're participating in some kind of 'internet meme' based on a newly-famous photo of some drugged-out pop star whose accidental traffic-related death had been captured on film by the paparazzi in L.A. Nice.

After a few hours I take a cab back to my hotel and get blotto in the downstairs bar. I meet a couple of tourists from Minnesota and I pretend to know about hockey for a few minutes even though I've never watched a game in my life; then I feel my zComm begin to vibrate and I'm suddenly an expert on the sport. Also: The art of juggling predates all recorded history, making its exact origins impossible to trace #themoreyouknow.

《《《——》》》

Some asshole's pounding on my door at seven in the morning and before I have time gather my senses and answer the thing Pavel's managed to pick the lock and let himself into my room. "Good morning," he says dryly.

"Yo. How's it going, Pavel?"

"We will order room service for breakfast and then depart for Kazan."

"Okay then. MetoTech's paying so let's order up a feast. Sound good?"

"Da."

«««—»»»

Pavel cranks his classical music CD full blast for two hours before I get frustrated and switch it off. He gives me a dirty look and I ask him how much longer the drive is going to be. "Another eight hours," he says. "Depending on traffic."

"Super," I moan, staring blankly into the ominously grey skyline smothering us and the rest of this godforsaken country. *No reward is worth this.*

Pavel's smartphone starts to vibrate and he checks the caller ID to see who it is. He looks at me and asks me something in a language I don't understand, probably Georgian or Ukrainian or something. When he sees I can't compute what he's saying he answers the phone and talks to whoever's on the other line in that same language for a while. Prick.

«««—»»»

We stop for gas and food in a place called Cheboksary and I freak out for a second before I realize that it isn't the village that was accidentally nuked back in the eighties. Pavel tells me we're going to eat first and pulls into a not-bad looking diner overlooking the highway. After an emaciated teenager shows us to our table Pavel orders us two bowls of something called Okroshka and goes to use the bathroom.

As soon as he's gone I start to think about how I wish I knew more European languages so I knew what the fuck Pavel had been talking about back in the car and then a custom ring tone starts to emanate from somewhere and after a few seconds I realize it's the same TV theme melody that Miller was whistling back in Albany. I start to feel dizzy and then all of a sudden the room's spinning completely out of control. I try to stand up but a violent vertigo assails my senses and I end up grasping the edges of our table while trying excruciatingly-hard not to vomit. Then the gay ringtone stops and everything instantly goes back to normal. I sit back down in my chair and down a whole glass of water. My nerves are shot to hell.

Pavel reappears and sits back down in front of me. He instantly starts telling me about how he'd tracked some drug dealer to a hideout near here back when he was in the FSB. I'm not really paying attention to the story and he notices the bored look in my eyes and starts to get angry. Luckily the waitress brings us our soup before he says anything further.

«««—»»»

After a few more hours driving it occurs to me to ask Pavel about this lead we're chasing and he laughs gruffly. "Yes, I suppose I am obliged to inform you of these things." He's quite good at sounding very official, very Russian. Pavel tells me with a 'dramatic inflection' that a former associate of his from the secret police recently received a tip from someone at Interpol that this dude named Horace Conrad is currently hiding out at some fancy hotel in Kazan.

I ask Pavel what this Conrad guy has to do with MetroTech's search for the Spartak Trigger and he looks over at me like I'm retarded. "I take it, American, that you are rather new to the intelligence game, yes?"

"Da."

Pavel sighs and explains to me that Conrad founded some website called InfoSpill that leaked all kinds of classified government documents to the public last year as part of the International Association of Workers' not-so-secret attempt to instigate instability in the world's leading capitalist countries. I think about asking him what the International Association of Workers is exactly but think better of it. Luckily the narrator chimes in and explains to us that it's a 'multinational conglomerate of various anarcho-syndicalist labor unions and ultra-left wing political parties.' Then he starts to sound kind of sleepy as he goes on to dispassionately describe Pavel's erratic driving style.

«««—»»»

We finally get to Kazan and I ask Pavel if Conrad is liable to have the Spartak Trigger on him and he loudly slaps his forehead with an open palm, disgusted. "No," he chides. "Conrad is just a disaffected intellectual worm. He would have no idea that the Spartak Trigger even exists."

"Then why the fuck did we drive ten hours to talk to him?"

"Because—he could very well know where we can find the splintered extremist faction of the I.A.W. who we believe *does* have the microfilm we're after. Or, at the very least, he will know where we can find someone else who might know where they are."

"Okay, gotcha, cool. Let's roll."

We get out of the car and look up at the luxurious hotel this champagne socialist radical is hiding out at, both of us clearly impressed. Pavel gets another call on his smartphone and this time I can understand him clearly so I guess I learned a bunch more language back in Cheboksary. He tells whoever he's talking to that he's at the hotel now and that he'll call them back after he interrogates Conrad and "eliminates the American nuisance." Nice.

As soon as Pavel hangs up I ask him the name of the splintered faction of the I.A.W. that he thinks has the microfilm and he tells me. I ask him what Conrad's room number is and he tells me that as well, albeit with a heavy dosage of attitude. We enter the hotel through the back entrance and a young security guard gives us a hard time but Pavel gets me to slip the guy a few Euros and it's all good. The kid even gives us his business card.

When we're in a dark metallic staircase Pavel whips out a pair of pistols fixed with silencers. "There is a strong possibility Conrad will have armed bodyguards with him." He hands me one of the guns. "Take this, American. You do know how to use a gun I trust?" His tone is overtly-condescending.

"Well, let's see." I flick the safety off with my thumb and shoot Pavel in the chest at point blank range. He grunts and drops to the ground like a sack of hammers. I spit on his body as I step over it on my way up the staircase. *Piece of shit rapist...*

<<<—>>>

I bang my fist on Conrad's door and a barrage of derogatory language is hurled my way in a thick English accent. Most of what the guy's yelling seems to be comprised of British slang terms that I've only ever heard in movies and late-1970's punk rock songs. I wait a moment and then knock again.

The second time I knock Conrad calmly tells me to leave him alone so then I break the door down with a swift shoulder check. Conrad's only wearing a white bath robe and he looks like he hasn't seen daylight in months. His paunchy frame and long, disheveled hair make him look like anything but the super-dangerous 'digital terrorist' the narrator claims he's been made out to be. I quickly survey the premises and see that he's alone.

"Who the bollocks are you?" he demands, anxiously. I tell him I'm only here to ask him a few questions and then I'll be on my way.

"Who sent you?" he demands.

"Why are you here by yourself?" I fire back.

"I asked you first."

"I have a gun."

"Good point." A cunning smirk prances across Conrad's pasty, high-planed face. "Well we may as well sit down I suppose." The world-famous fugitive motions for me to have a seat at one of the stools situated adjacent to a densely-lacquered oak bar as the narrator quickly lists all of the room's first-class amenities. "Nice place you've got here," I offer as I lean against the bar with my gun still pointed at Conrad's head.

"Thanks." He stops himself from sitting down in mid-crouch. "Can I offer you something to drink?"

I tell him sure and he proceeds to mix us a couple of martinis. He hands me mine and I chug the thing back. It's got a decent kick to it. He sighs and tells me that patience is a virtue so I call him a homo and ask him again why he's hiding out here without a bodyguard or anything.

"There's actually a very good reason for that." He takes a sip from his martini and starts to compliment himself on the expertise with which he'd mixed the fucking drink. I fire a stealth-sounding round off, knocking a bowl of wax fruit from its perch atop an abnormally-high coffee table. That gets his attention.

"I couldn't trust anyone anymore, okay?" he blurts out, hysterically. "That's why I'm alone now. My own people betrayed me, sold me out to the authorities to save themselves from a few fines for fucking tax evasion. They set me up to take the fall on the whole InfoSpill thing even though I was never directly involved. I'm like Oswald man—just a patsy!"

I tell Conrad to calm down and that I don't give two shits about him or his gay website or his stupid cause. "You can die of scurvy right here in this hotel room for all I care," I tell him candidly.

"Then why are you here?" he asks, confused.

"I'm here because I've been led to believe that you might know where I can find a group of anarchists that call themselves Black October."

Conrad's face goes grey and he starts to tremble unsubtly. He reaches into his robe pocket and pulls out a small pipe that he fumbles with for a moment before dropping on the white-tiled floor. "Where did you hear of Black October?" he asks me, his voice 'suffused with panic.'

"They have in their possession a certain item that the people I work for desperately wish to obtain." I flick the safety back on and start spinning Pavel's pistol around my finger like a cocky gunslinger in some corny Western movie. "An associate of mine received a tip that you were staying here and that you might be able to steer me in the right direction, given that you were previously affiliated with the I.W.A. at the same time as Black October's principle members."

"You mean the I.A.W?"

"Yeah, sure. Whatever. Them too."

Conrad's 'façade of alarm' has vanished, replaced by a shrewd, conniving look. "What do they have that you want so badly?" he asks. I narrow my eyes and stop spinning the gun. It's once again aimed at Conrad's head.

"Black October," I growl. "Where are they?"

"Well if you kill me you'll never find them, will you, Mister…"

"Markov. Sergei Markov."

"An exotic name for an American. Your accent isn't quite perfect by the way—you might want to work on that."

"Thanks for the tip. You can call me Mitchell then. Pete Mitchell."

"Well, now that we know each other's names and have had a drink together I'd say we're well on our way to becoming best friends, what do you say?"

I try to stay in character but the guy's pretty charming and I realize that he's probably the only person in the world who's in a more fucked up position than me at the moment so that's cool I guess. "Fine, we're friends, whatever. Now where the hell can I find these Black October assholes?"

"I'll tell you what, Sergei Markov slash Pete Mitchell. I'll *show* you where they are!" Conrad exuberantly raises his arms in the air, causing his robe to reveal his ample belly and a pair of bright orange boxer shorts. His sagging chest is littered with patches of hair and his bony little legs appear to offer little in the way of structural support. "I really need to get out of here. If you've tracked me down word of my whereabouts is bound to spread…"

I cock my wrist threateningly and tell Conrad to refasten his robe, which he does with great haste. He tells me he really should get dressed anyway, since we'll be leaving soon. I nod reluctantly and he giddily dashes into the adjoining bedroom.

"So how far is it to where Black October's hiding?" I yell, turning on the room's plasma television. Footage of the North Korean Army training at some massive base is being shown on some bullshit European news station. Conrad doesn't answer me. "Looks like these gooks are getting wound up about something," I announce.

Conrad reemerges donning a bizarre costume that the narrator describes as being a cross between a Celtic troubadour and a Norwegian lumberjack.

"What the hell are you wearing?" I ask, dumfounded.

"Well I can't very well travel incognito now, can I—a world famous fugitive such as myself!"

"It's not that hard to pull off. Trust me. Put on some normal clothes or I'll just, like, torture you until you tell me what I want to know."

"Very well, but I'll have you know that this outfit has come in quite handy since I've been on the lamb. You'd be surprised how easily the international police are thrown off by simple misdirection—sleight of mind if you will. It's actually an interesting phenomenon, originating in a school of thought from -"

I fire a round into the wall. "Shut up and get changed already."

«‹‹—›»

Brooding with supernatural calm, Bishop checks the hallway carefully before motioning for Conrad to follow him back down the corridor. They glide across an authentic Savonnerie carpet, past a series of discarded room service trays. Conrad stops in front of the elevators but Bishop quickly grabs him by the shoulders and pulls him into a poorly-lit stairwell. The duo descend the steps with tremendous haste, stopping only long enough for Bishop to retrieve a second gun and a set of car keys from the motionless corpse of the elephantine ex-FSB officer he'd disposed of earlier.

Bishop whispers an overtly-sarcastic "dasvidaniya" to Pavel as he leaves the body behind and drags a shocked Horace Conrad down the remainder of the stairs and out into the hotel parking lot.

Conrad begins hyperventilating and tries to ask his abductor about what happened to the dead man they've just robbed. "Don't worry about it," Bishop jibes, caustically. "It doesn't matter." He shoves Conrad into their inherited sedan and starts ridiculing me about several of the words I've elected to use in relaying their hurried evacuation of the scene. His body odor still rank and his testicles still shriveled and tiny, Bishop fires up the car's engine and peels out of the lot like a lead-footed teenager.

«««—»»»

As soon as we start driving I ask Conrad a few questions and quickly realize that he's somewhat exaggerated his knowledge of Black October's whereabouts. When I call him out on it he just chuckles uneasily and says all he really knows is the name of the town in Russia they're liable to be found in. I ask him what the odds are they'll be there he thinks for a minute and says they're better than average.

"Good enough," I say. "Just how dangerous are these guys anyhow?"

"Very. They're not our biggest problem at the moment though."

"Well then what is?"

"The man with the machine gun leaning out of the side door of the cargo van we're currently heading towards."

«««—»»»

The pussy driving the oncoming van drives into a ditch after I pull into his lane and hammer my accelerator even though his vehicle's twice the size of mine. Conrad's still screaming at me in all kinds of different languages and slamming his hands excitedly into the dashboard long after I've pulled back into the proper lane. I calmly remind him that the "chicken game" maneuver worked to perfection and that shuts him up eventually.

"You think those guys were after you?" I ask Conrad, who I'm pretty sure has pissed his pants.

"No…well, maybe. Could they have been coming after you?"

"Maybe."

"Or maybe they weren't coming after either of us."

"Yeah, I suppose that's also a possibility."

"So then you just ran a van occupied by at least one man brandishing an automatic weapon off the road for no reason?"

"Whatever dude—I saw a potentially hazardous situation and diffused it, stop being such a little bitch about it."

I ask Conrad which direction I should go once we get on the freeway and he tells me east. "How far?" I demand.

"Only about eighteen-hundred kilometers. Should take us a day or so tops." Super.

«««—»»»

Conrad talks non-stop for almost the entire drive to Omsk. He gives me his whole friggin' life story starting with how he'd dropped out of some fancy university back in the UK after his parents died and left him a massive inheritance. Pissed off at the government for some reason, he hired a bunch of teenaged computer nerds to start hacking into various state-run networks to commit random acts of digital sabotage. "You probably heard of the great Notting Hill blackout of ninety-eight?"

"Nope, can't say that I have."

"What? Come on—it was a huge story!" I just shrug and my passenger is somehow offended that the mainstream American press didn't allocate more coverage to a power outage in a small district of a foreign city twenty years ago.

Conrad lets it go and goes on to tell me that after a few years of causing mischief like that he was recruited by the British chapter of the International Association of Workers. They wanted him and his legion of technological ne'er-do-wells to use their computer skills to wreak havoc upon several international financial institutions as a means of destabilizing the capitalist agenda or something. "I didn't give a fuck about their politics—I just wanted to see if we could do it," he implores. "The next thing I know the I.A.W. has completely honed in on my operation and they started doing all kinds of shit without my knowing, all the while making public statements about adapting the tactics of guerilla warfare to the information age… That's when they launched InfoSpill and claimed that I was the mastermind behind it. They even put a photo of me on the main page's goddamn masthead"

I ask Conrad why the I.A.W. used him as their front man for the site and he tells me it was because he'd come from a privileged family and had allegedly grown to embrace the ideology of anarcho-socialism. The fact that he'd rejected the principles of capitalism, even after having reaped its benefits, made his story a great propaganda tool despite the fact that he didn't actually know anything about politics and didn't give a "toss" about socialism. The narrator takes this as a cue to launch into a lecture about the evolution of socialism in the post-industrial/information age and I yell at him to stop so he starts telling more lies about my B.O. and shit. Asshole.

"When did they sell you out to the authorities then?" I ask a 'disconcerted' Conrad.

The Brit takes a few seconds before he responds, the answer obviously still upsetting to him. "As soon as InfoSpill started leaking documents about the Central Intelligence Agency's involvement in the Egyptian Revolution of 2011 the I.A.W. started to feel a lot of heat from the U.N. Security Council."

Conrad's starting to sound an awful lot like The Wizard and the narrator even acknowledges certain similarities between the two characters. "They demanded the site be shut down and threatened to come down hard on the Secretary General of the I.A.W. since they'd been openly running the site and all. So, he and the other two members of the Secretariat go and claim that I'd gone rogue on them and had been running InfoSpill without their knowledge the whole time, can you believe that shit?"

"Sure, I'd do the same thing," I tell him.

"Of course you would. I probably would as well come to think of it... At any rate, I managed to get out of England with the aid of some I.A.W. members who'd disagreed with the Secretariat's position and I've been hiding out here in Russia ever since..."

"And who was paying for you to stay at that palace back in Kazan?" I ask.

"My old public school roommate actually. His older brother owns that hotel and a hundred others like it in Eastern Europe, got in right after the wall came down and made a fortune. He owed me a favor since I'd helped him cheat on Part One of his DSA exam."

"I thought you said there wasn't anyone left you could trust?" I'm not sure the derisiveness of my tone is warranted.

"Well there are a few exceptions I suppose."

I tell Conrad about Pavel's connection at Interpol and how he'd missed being arrested by a matter of hours. He cowers for a moment before thanking me for inadvertently rescuing him.

"Don't mention it. Now. Tell me how these Black October assholes fit into all of this bullshit?"

Conrad's face turns to stone and he stares out the window for a long time before answering. "There are only a handful of them," he says. "But they're the most dangerous gang of psychos the I.A.W.'s paramilitary division ever produced. After their first few assignments they couldn't be controlled and when the Secretariat tried to break them up they just quit and started their

THE SPARTAK TRIGGER

own organization which has allegedly been responsible for dozens of bombings at financial institutions all over Europe. They've also been known to kidnap and torture prominent conservative politicians in rather…sadistic fashion."

"Interesting. What else do you know about these guys?"

"Their leader claims tó be a descendent of Nestor Makhno, who led an army of anarchists against the Bolsheviks shortly after the Russian Revolution."

Okay. "Okay." So I guess The Wizard wasn't totally right and the jacket copy is just plain wrong. Whatever.

"This kid is bonkers, absolutely mental," Conrad says. "I only ever met him one time—at the Sixth International Conference in Geneva a few years back. He was thrown out after loudly accusing the Secretary General of the I.A.W. of being an undercover MI-6 agent sent to keep the far left from unifying through intentionally-ineffective leadership. He broke off and formed Black October a few days later."

"I thought you said they were expelled from the I.A.W.?"

"Did I?"

"Pretty sure you did."

We pass the scene of an accident, both of us recoiling subtly when the officer on the scene makes eye contact with us as we coast by.

"Ah well, my mistake. Sorry about that Pete."

"It's fine. So how do you know they're now based out of Omsk exactly?"

"To be totally honest it's just a rumor I'd heard when I was still in the I.A.W."

"Great. Just great. A fucking rumor is what we're going on?"

"Have you got anything better?"

I ignore Conrad's question and turn the radio on, cranking some kickass Euro metal up full blast.

《《《—》》》

By the time we get to Omsk's desolate outskirts I'm about ready to strangle Conrad and save the international courts a great deal of time and money. He's been going on for hours about how in the near-future mass media will be entirely user-generated which will help form a "hive-like collective consciousness that could easily propagate a supernova-level Abilene paradox" even though I've told him multiple times that I don't care about any of this. The narrator tells us that Conrad's totally ambivalent to the passive aggressive hostility I've been exhibiting so I outright tell the guy I don't like him and his mouth falls open in shock.

I proceed to announce that we're going into the seediest bar we can find in the city and that I'm going to try and get some information from its patrons. *Always works in movies, what the hell.* Then I explain—rather firmly—that Conrad is absolutely forbidden from speaking to anyone once we're in there. He must be thinking about Pavel's carcass back at the hotel in Kazan because he agrees without protest. The final twenty-odd minutes of our drive is spent in a glorious silence as both the narrator and MetroTech miraculously decide to leave me alone as well.

«««—»»»

Omsk has the 'bombastic cheerlessness' of most any blue collar city in the American Midwest so I decide pretty quickly that just about any bar outside of the downtown core will have the kind of lowlife customers we're looking to meet. After we pass what looks like a shopping district and a couple of neoclassical cathedrals I spot a place that looks like it's on the verge of being condemned and tell Conrad that we're going in. He asks me if he can just stay in the car and I tell him no.

"Why not?" he protests.

"Because I hate drinking alone even more than I hate you right now."

THE SPARTAK TRIGGER

«««—»»»

I order us two pints of Krepkoe and the one-armed bartender gives me a curious look, like I'm a complete stranger asking for his daughter's hand in marriage or something. He charges me more than the price they've got listed on a dust-covered placard but I don't say anything and give him a generous tip.

We grab a seat in a darkened area of the tavern. Conrad tells me he doesn't much care for lager and I tell him to shut the fuck up and drink it. After a few rounds I'm starting to feel pretty good and start to engage in some playful banter with a couple of drunken rowdies who appear to be regulars.

The two guys are about my age and celebrating one of their birthdays so I buy them both a shot of vodka and all of a sudden they're my best friends. Just as I'm buying another round of beers for Conrad and myself, a group of severe, young-looking dudes saunter on into the bar and everyone in whole place stops talking in unison as an eerie silence swiftly engulfs the joint. My new pals suddenly both have a look of visceral, primal fear in their eyes and I guess I've found what I'm looking for.

The truculent party of twenty-somethings strolls purposefully across the room and lays claim to a table close to where Conrad's hunched over. I quickly pay for our drinks and rejoin him. Several people leave the place as soon as the tri-limbed barkeep sends a kid that looks like he's about twelve over to take the new arrivals' order.

Conrad's about ready to pass out when I nudge him with my elbow and tell him to perk up because we're open for business. He mumbles something about Manchester United and gets up to take a piss, knocking his chair over in the process.

"You should get your friend home," the smallest occupant of the table next to us shouts in my direction. "He could get into trouble being so inebriated in a place such as this." I estimate that this guy is their leader since the others all laugh phonily at what I guess is supposed to be a joke. I tell the dick to mind his own business and he doesn't like that. Not one bit. He's handsome in a Hollywood villain kind of way, with a maniacal glimmer in his bright blue eyes that reminds me of...something.

The bartender sees that I've upset his most dangerous customers and rushes over to me to tell me to get out. I loudly tell him I'm looking for a group that calls themselves Black October and the tavern's handicapped proprietor immediately sulks back into the shadows as the two largest members of the drearily-dressed horde sitting across from me stand and roll their sleeves up to reveal identical tattoos—a black capital "A" encased within a circle—emblazoned upon all four of their massive, ghost white biceps. Their vibrantly-pale arms contrast sharply with the bar's murky lighting scheme.

The narrator sheepishly apologizes for what he calls a 'contrived coincidence' as the smaller, good-looking guy tells me that I've just met Black October and his body builder friends advance upon me. My zComm starts to hum with urgency and the narrator has to apologize again—this time for invoking some Latin-sounding plot device, day-us somethingorother, as a few seconds later I'm a world-class martial artist. Cool.

I resist the urge to quote a famous line from a popular late-nineties science fiction movie after using kung fu to incapacitate both of my attackers within a matter of seconds, my hands and feet a 'whirlwind of lethality.' After both men are lying on the floor unconscious, the two remaining Black October underlings pull out pistols and point them at me in unison exactly as I draw both of Pavel's handguns.

The alpha male amongst them laughs scathingly and tells me to take a seat. I put my guns away and his compatriots do likewise. I look around and notice that the tavern is now completely deserted.

"My name is Kirill," Black October's de facto leader tells me as soon as I'm seated. "These are my associates Alexei and Alexei." His two henchmen nod at me formally. I introduce myself as Peter Mitchell, in English. Kirill asks me how I knew to find him here. "I have my sources," I lie.

THE SPARTAK TRIGGER

"Very well, Peter Mitchell." Kirill's English is surprisingly good. "Tell me though. Why is it that you seek to find an audience with my organization?"

I tell Kirill that until recently I was a member of an American-based anarcho-communist group called the Worker's Liberation Front. "The leaders of the W.L.F. decided to join into the wretched I.A.W., at which point I denounced them and sought out to find a new party whose philosophies were more in line with my way of thinking. All I knew of Black October is that it had split from the I.A.W. due to ideological differences, and that their leader was a descendent of the great Nestor Makhno."

This last statement seems to pique Kirill's interest. "Ah, so you are a Makhnovist," he says with glee. "My great grandfather was indeed a brilliant man and a tremendous leader." The members of Black October who are still conscious gaze at him with identical looks of brazen adoration. "As are you, Kirill," the Alexei to his left says.

"That remains to be seen," Kirill replies, humorlessly.

I lean back in my chair, hoping to hell that Kirill doesn't ask me to explain what I like about Makhnovism exactly. Just as he gets ready to say something else the door to the bar swings open and the most beautiful woman I've ever seen is standing in the doorway, her figure seemingly illuminated by some kind of paranormal light source. "Darling!" Kirill exclaims, standing up and walking over to meet her.

They embrace ceremoniously and he kisses her gently upon the lips. She removes her winter hat and a gorgeous array of auburn hairs descend upon her shoulders, perfectly framing an angelic face upon which a bright, breathtaking smile is garlanded.

"This is my fiancée—Svetlana," Kirill announces as he escorts the goddess over to our table. "Meet Peter Mitchell—an American who is loyal to our cause and wishes to join our ranks."

I stand up and shake her hand, managing to avoid eye contact out of fear of becoming any further enchanted. "Very nice to meet you," Svetlana tells me in broken English.

"Mister Mitchell actually speaks Russian quite well," Kirill says as we all sit back down. "Very rare for a Westerner. Very rare indeed. Where did you learn our language exactly?"

"Mostly from watching *Nu, pogodi!* cartoons," I tell him, remembering an old Soviet-era show I'd seen a documentary about at some point.

"Ah yes, a true classic of the genre." Kirill diabolically steeples his fingers as the lower half of his face contorts itself into a 'devious sneer.' "The hare, he is very clever in this program—always one step ahead of the wolf."

"What happened to Mikhail and Vasiliy?" Svetlana asks coolly as she lights a cigarette.

"Don't worry about them dear, they're just taking a nap," Kirill says, facetiously. He motions for Svetlana to hand him a cigarette before turning to face me wielding a perplexed expression. "Speaking of which, what on earth has become of your intoxicated companion, Peter?"

"Good question. Will you excuse me a moment?" I stand up and walk into the bathroom where I find Conrad sprawled out along a filthy floor, his arms wrapped around a vomit-covered toilet. "Lightweight," I mutter, grabbing him by the shoulders and propping him up with surprising ease. "Get it together, man. We're in good with these assholes."

Conrad starts to come around after a few seconds and curses me out for making him drink so much. "Suck it up, buttercup." I punch my pseudo-partner in the shoulder and he starts to giggle deliriously.

«««—»»»

It takes us about an hour to drive out to Black October's secret hideout. It's snowing quite heavily now plus I'm pretty drunk so I almost lose Kirill a couple of times after we plunge into a dark, densely-wooded area pierced by a single, narrow lane. Conrad seems annoyed that nobody in Omsk has recognized

THE SPARTAK TRIGGER

him yet, which I suppose is pretty weird considering he's allegedly been all over the news for the past few months and he'd met Kirill at that pinko festival a few years ago. Allegedly. I promise to try and casually bring up his celebrity status once we get to the bad/good/whatever guys' stronghold.

《《《—》》》

The modest bungalow Black October calls home is surprisingly unsightly, even for a small gang of insurgent anarchist revolutionaries. Conrad talks everyone's ear off once we get inside their rundown refuge after I nonchalantly mention the InfoSpill scandal. Kirill doesn't remember meeting Conrad but is well aware of the fact that he'd broken ties with the I.A.W. in a hostile manner so that buys us some extra cred thankfully.

Pretty soon after we've gotten settled Conrad's managed to instigate a heated dogmatic discussion littered with philosophical posturing and other such nonsense. I'm doing my best to act like I know what the fuck they're talking about as outlandish terms like "platorism" and "freigeld" are tossed around like beanbags at a hacky sack convention. I survey Conrad's 'mendacious visage' with extreme distrust as he appears to have lied to me about not really caring about politics. *Why would he do that?*

I step outside for some fresh air when I can't take any more pretentious-sounding rhetoric.

Once I'm alone in the oppressively-cold winter air I say aloud that I wish I knew more about this anarchist shit and the tingling sensation in the back of my head returns. The complete history of revolutionary politics in Eastern Europe is wired into my brain almost instantaneously. I offer my masters halfhearted thanks as I gather my senses after the zComm shifts back into passive mode.

Svetlana appears out of nowhere and asks me if I'd like a cigarette. I politely decline, finally looking into her stunning, sapphire eyes as I do so. My heart skips a beat. "It's chilly out," I say, stupidly.

"It is not too bad," Kirill's fiancée replies. "What part of America do you come from, Peter?"

I tell her I'm from Grand Rapids, Michigan and she asks me if the winters are bad there. "Yeah," I say. "But not like this."

"Why don't you live in California then? If you don't like the cold weather that is."

"I don't know. Maybe I should."

Svetlana kind of gives me a flirty look as she lights her cigarette with an antique lighter. I feel like a stoned high-schooler for a few seconds as the narrator makes fun of himself for so flagrantly entering into what he refers to as a 'clumsy trope.' I ask Svetlana how she ended up getting involved with all of this and she tells me with a surprising sincerity that her family had been devastated twice by revolution—first by the Bolsheviks ninety years ago and again by the western-style reforms of the early 1990s—and she means to be on the front lines of the next social upheaval so as to avoid being blindsided once more.

I ask her what she means and she explains that her great grandparents had been pretty well off—"Kulaks"—before having had their land confiscated by the Soviets after the Reds won the Civil War. They were sent to a labor camp for good measure. Then, after two generations of dutifully following the communists' rigid platforms, the country gets flipped upside down yet again and blood thirsty gangsters seized control of all of the main industries…all of the resources. Everything.

"My father was loyal to the party for his whole life, worked hard in a tank factory for forty years." Svetlana takes a substantial drag from her cigarette. "Then when the coup against Gorbachev was successful he lost his job and was forced to borrow money from the criminals who took command of our city. He had no means to pay them back and eventually took his own life out of humiliation. My mother died of grief soon thereafter."

"Wow, that's awful."

"Yes. It is." There's a rugged vulnerability in Svetlana's voice that makes her even more appealing somehow. "Once the people rise up again against our oppressors and take back what is rightfully ours, my family will at long last have its revenge. This is all that I care about in this life, which is why I have dedicated myself to the principles of anarchism."

Just as I'm getting ready to ask Svetlana about how she met Kirill the door to Black October's shack swings open and one of the Alexeis tells me I need to come inside. "What is it?" I demand.

"You've got a phone call," he says.

"A phone call?"

"Yes."

I walk briskly into the shoddy edifice and Kirill's holding the body of an old-fashioned rotary phone in his right hand with the drawn receiver in his left. He's radiating 'acute suspicion' out of his 'severe, judicious' face and I reach for the receiver with extreme caution.

"Who on earth could possibly know I'm here?" I ask, confused beyond belief.

"That is interesting," Kirill says, icily. "I was thinking the exact same thing."

I take the phone and hold it to my ear. I notice the Alexeis both have rifles in their hands and appear ready to use them at the drop of a hat. I turn away from the group, as if that somehow magically produces a sound proof barrier between us.

"Hello?" I ask.

"Peter Mitchell?" a rigid, bureaucratic voice asks.

"Yes." My cardiac rhythm begins to speed up.

"Have you also used the alias Sergei Markov recently?" The deep voice's tone remains 'utterly stoical.'

"Yes."

"Prior to that were you known as Ryan Butler?"

"Yes." *Who the fuck is this??*

"And prior to that did you go by the name Jack Stone."

I can't breath. I can sense the rifles being raised and pointed at my back. "Yes."

"Before that did you use the name Terry Brelen?"

"I did." I look behind me and see Mikhail and Vasiliy both glaring at me intensely as they retrieve identical hunting knives from a large cupboard.

"And you used the alias Bernard Anthony Roberts prior to that?"

My heart's about ready to burst out of my chest. "That's correct."

"And you've also gone by the name Kyle Johnson at various times?"

"Uh-huh." I turn around and offer an exasperated shrug to my hosts, trying to show them that I'm just as alarmed and mystified as they are about the call I'm on.

"And your birth name is Shane Francis Bishop?"

"It is." The Alexeis' guns are now aimed at my head. I look helplessly towards a frightened Conrad.

"Terrific!" the intrusive stranger's voice suddenly becomes jovial and I nearly fall down in shock. "We've been trying to get ahold of you for quite some time, Mister Bishop."

"Who is this??" I'm back in character and sound like a badass once again.

"My name is Cedric and I'm very pleased to let you know that you've been selected as a candidate to become a member of the ultra-exclusive Super Budget Discount Rewards Club! For a limited time we are offering new associates a one-time-only introductory trial membership rate of just one dollar for the first month. Should you elect to remain in the Super Budget Discount Rewards Club after thirty days the standard membership rate of twenty-nine dollars per quarter will automatically be billed to your credit card ending in the digits five-three-oh-nine. By mercilessly ridiculing me with off-color language and then abruptly hanging up, your contract will automatically be activated and you will receive our welcome package in the mail within five-to-ten business days. Do you understand the terms of our agreement as I have read them to you?"

THE SPARTAK TRIGGER

"Nice try, Cedric." I shake my head in a reassuring manner and the scene relaxes slightly. Svetlana walks back inside and is instantly taken aback by the sight of her comrades brandishing weapons.

Cedric starts talking again. "Mister Bishop, since you've been so patient with me on this call I'm also pleased to let you know that if you agree to join the Super Budget Discount Rewards Club today we'll be sending you a complimentary Valued Partner booklet which contains over five hundred dollars in coupons redeemable at select merchants throughout the continental United States."

"You called me in Russia, dude."

"Right you are sir, and I'll remind you that the Super Budget Discount Rewards Club offers Valued Partners such as yourself extensive travel benefits such as access to several VIP lounges in select airports throughout North America, Europe, and parts of Asia."

"Wow, that's amazing."

Kirill takes out a pistol and fires a bullet into his own phone, promptly terminating my overseas call. "I fucking hate telemarketers," he says.

«‹‹—››»

Conrad and I have to share a small air mattress Black October bought at their only neighbors' recent yard sale. The bastard talks in his sleep and he's having a dream about riding a unicorn through a meadow or some shit. Pretty weird. Also pretty gay.

«‹‹—››»

Kirill is up at the crack of dawn and he takes me with him to retrieve some supplies from town. After his car's engine finally turns over on his third attempt he tells me that Black October is planning something big that will require a lot of money to finance. I ask him how much money we're talking about and he tells me a hundred thousand Euros. "That's not all that much really," I tell him.

"Well it is about ninety-nine thousand more than we have at present," he retorts. "It's too bad your rich British friend has had his assets seized by his government, he would have had that sum a hundred-fold I'm sure."

"Yeah, probably." I scratch my forehead. "Just how big is this 'thing' you're talking about anyhow?"

"The complete annihilation of capitalism," Kirill says resolutely. "The propagation of an anarcho-socialist society that will flourish all over the globe. This is what Black October will accomplish once we obtain these funds I speak of."

I pretend like I'm both impressed and surprised for a few seconds. "How exactly do you propose to achieve this monumental undertaking?"

Kirill's youthful face becomes furtive and he raises his thin eyebrows expectantly as a focused, wily look invades his eyes. "I cannot tell you right now, Peter. You have yet to earn my trust implicitly."

"Fair enough." I roll down my window and spit out a blood-tinted globule. "What can I do to accomplish that? I'll do anything for our cause, Kirill, you know that. I've come halfway around the world just to meet you for crying out loud." I roll my window back up.

"This is true. And both you and your computer-savvy friend can definitely be of value to us moving forward. However, in order for me to know that you are a man we can trust to help bring about the coming revolution, you must do something for me."

"Name it."

Kirill pulls over to the side of the road and turns to address me in a very official capacity. "I have learned that a local narcotics dealer will be making a large transaction with one of his suppliers later tonight," he tells me. "My source estimates that at least five million rubles will exchange hands."

"How many Euros is that?"

"One hundred, twenty-four thousand, seven hundred and twenty-three."

"Nice chunk of change. So you want me to rob this drug dealer for you?"

"Yes. That's exactly what I want. Perform this task for us and we will anoint you a full member of Black October. Your name will appear in the history books alongside that of the world's most powerful Anarch"

"Conrad too?"

"Conrad too."

"Your wish is my command, comrade."

"Excellent, the deal is supposed to take place at midnight tonight at an abandoned military compound along the Irtysh River. The parties involved will not suspect an ambush, and a single man with your…lethal skillset and obvious combat experience should be able to get the jump on them with relative ease."

"Okay."

Just as I've almost forgotten what I'm doing here that irritating TV theme song bleeps into my head and I remember all too well that I'm on a mission of a different kind that needs to be completed sooner than later. "Do you know where this drug dealer lives?" I ask.

"Yes. He has a flat in the Kirovsky district."

"Take me there this morning then. He's liable to have the money with him already and it would be better to take him on alone before his supplier becomes involved."

Kirill smiles. "You Americans are all so…what's the expression. Gung ho?"

"Fuck yeah."

«‹‹—›››

Kirill cranks some annoying techno music and I pretend to like it as we speed towards a Russian criminal's apartment in some random part of Omsk I'll hopefully never have to set foot in again. Black October's company car is a real jalopy but it still moves pretty quickly when Kirill shifts up a few gears.

I take out the pistols I stole from Pavel back in Kazan and make sure they're loaded as we pull up to a Soviet-style housing unit flanked by a pair of crumbling office buildings. I ask Kirill what kind of shit this guy peddles and he tells me mainly cocaine and heroin. "What's the apartment number?" I ask with the 'swash buckling bluster of a silent film-era action star.' *Really? Wow...*

"Twenty-four. Be careful."

Whatever. "Whatever."

The narrator paints an unflattering portrait of a man detached from anything remotely resembling a discernible human condition as I make my way across the street and into the mark's place of residence. I bump into a young couple on my way up the stairs and they curse at me using a bunch of fucked up Russian slang that I guess MetroTech didn't think I needed to know.

I knock on Apartment 24's decaying wooden door and an unfriendly voice asks me what I want. "Just looking for a quick fix," I plead, trying to sound like a Russian junky.

"Get the fuck out of here," the door demands.

I beg the guy for a gram of coke, using a pathetic, sniveling voice that I've heard dozens of addicts use over the years. Apartment 24's spokesman tells me to leave right now or there will be trouble for me and I tell him I can't leave until I score some coke. I can hear some other voices mingling inside and all of a sudden I'm outnumbered. Great. *At least they think you're just some drug-ravaged weakling.* Good point.

The door creeps open and a hard-looking asshole in a wool winter hat peers at me through an unfeeling pair of eyes for a second or two before he realizes that I'm not a junky and yells out another Russian word I don't know. I take out one of my guns and shoot him square in the forehead. I kick open the door and see the apartment's other two inhabitants each scrambling to grab one of the dozen-odd machine guns littered haphazardly throughout the spacious studio. I dive into the place headfirst, my guns stretching out before me, blazing. I'm suspended in mid-air until I've emptied both of my clips and then gravity drops me onto the floor. Ouch.

A 'sentient quietude' overtakes the scene as I get up and see that the bastards are both dead. I hurriedly scour the drug lair for a duffle bag or something that could carry a large amount of cash. The narrator eloquently conveys the torrent of urgency suddenly occupying me as he politely asks for your continued suspension of disbelief.

After tearing through the place I find several stacks of cash and a bag of coke hidden inside a kid's cereal box and make a beeline for Kirill's shitmobile. He fires up the engine as soon as he sees me emerge from the complex. I leap into the passenger seat and tell him to get us the fuck out of dodge. We race down the vacant city street and once I'm sure there isn't anyone following us I start to count the cash.

"That's a lot of money!" Kirill exclaims, looking over at my haul.

"No shit, Sherlockov." I take out the bag of coke I also swiped from Apartment 24 and take a generous snort as Kirill looks on, horrified. "So tell me how we're going to change the world, comrade," I demand. "Now that I've earned your trust *and* gotten you the money you need to make it happen that is."

«««—»»»

When we get back to the base Kirill tells everyone to give the two of us some privacy. Svetlana and the boys take a walk but I insist that Conrad stays and Kirill allows it.

My British friend gives me a confused, apprehensive look but I whisper that there's nothing to worry about and he instantly seems at ease, as if his faith in my judgment is implicit. Idiot. Kirill marches around the bungalow's small kitchenette for a while, his pace quickening with each step, as if he's winding himself up.

"What you are about to hear only a few people in the entire world are privy to," he proclaims in Wagnerian fashion. "You both know full well, especially you Conrad, that contemporary society is more dependent upon information than any other resource—a collective addiction perhaps more dramatic than in the history of humankind. More than oil, coal, and every other fossil fuel combined!" Kirill's delivery has ascended to a 'melodramatic crescendo' with remarkable rapidity.

He goes on to tell us pretty much the same cloak-and-dagger Russian spy conspiracy story Miller told me back in Albany. His version has a few minor contextual differences littered throughout, such as that the fact that the microfilm is currently stashed in a safety deposit box in Budapest and that he'd originally received it from an uncle of his who'd been an aid to a Politburo member. Conrad's mouth is hanging wide open well before Kirill gets to the part about his having recently made arrangements to hire an underground hacklab in Salzburg to refurbish a second generation computer that we can use to activate the Spartak Trigger after picking it up in Hungary. He also mentions that he has to wire the engineers their money before they'll give him the exact location of their special pre-magnetic memory core, transistor-based device.

"The price we negotiated was for a hundred thousand Euros," Kirill says, giving me a nod of thanks that I respond to with an enthusiastic, wink-enhanced 'thumbs-up' gesture. I think about asking Kirill if he'd ever communicated with anyone at the hacklab in Austria about this whole thing over Chirrup but I can't be bothered. *Sorry, Wiz.*

Conrad's even more hyper than usual now and he leaps up out of his seat and begins asking himself a series of rapid fire questions that he instantly answers back to himself, delineating as to whether or not what Kirill has told us is possible. They're mostly technobabble questions so I guess he also knows a lot more about that shit than he'd previously alluded to as well. Fucker. He starts going on about the chaos that took place in

THE SPARTAK TRIGGER

Egypt when the government shut the internet down and Kirill tells him that that was nothing compared to the forthcoming end of the World…Wide Web.

Black October's leader strikes a heroic, Lenin-statue-like pose and proclaims that from the chaos he will unleash upon the world, a new society founded upon the ansoc theology his great grandfather had developed a hundred years ago will arise.

"How do you plan to keep the leaders of the I.A.W. from becoming a part of this new social order?" I ask, pragmatically.

"Simple," Kirill states, almost aloofly. "After completing our impending mission, we proceed to stage an immediate coup and oust the Secretariat from power. We will then proclaim ourselves to be the *new* leaders of the International Association of Workers. I of course will assume the role of Secretary General, and lead the entire world into a socialist utopia that will last a millennium!"

"Rock and roll," I say, finally realizing how friggin' weird it is that all of these "anarchist" groups are so well-organized. "When do we leave for Hungary?"

Kirill takes his car keys out of his pocket and jostles them playfully. "Immediately."

«««—»»»

We drive over to a super-sketchy car dealership and trade in Pavel's sedan, Kirill's beater, and a fair bit of cash for a brand new, spacious van that all seven of us can fit in comfortably and we leave Omsk shortly thereafter. The drab morning sky insists upon saturating the horizon with a 'supple mist' that the narrator refers to ad nauseam throughout the first hour of our westward journey.

«««—»»»

We pose as soccer—or "football" as they call it on this stupid continent—fans at the border and I'm pretty pissed that the left-over rubles from my score are wasted on jerseys and face paints and shit but the customs agent happens to be a fan of whatever club we're meant to be supporting so he lets us pass into the Ukraine with such ease that it defies logic, fridge logic even.

The narrator does an awful job of justifying how the exact same ploy works when we cross the Hungarian border and when I call him out on being so flagrantly indolent everyone in the car looks at me like I'm crazy. Fair enough.

《《《—》》》

Right after we pass a marker that tells us that Budapest is only thirty-two kilometers away Kirill gives us a play-by-play account of him checking our fuel level and then he announces that we need gas—aka "petrol"—so he pulls into a "filling station." Svetlana and I are the only ones who have to use the bathroom so the others stay back in the van and we make our way over to the dilapidated convenience store.

The grizzled, mustachioed clerk looks like a fucking pervert and he gives Svetlana one of the creepiest once-overs I've ever seen when he hands us the restroom keys. I shoot him my trademark foreboding glare and he goes back to taking inventory of their tobacco products. I hold the door open and let Svetlana walk ahead of me so I can check out her immaculate ass, which is being put on display in awesome fashion by a pair of skin-tight thermal pants. "See you back at the van," I say, rather pointlessly, as she disappears into the women's washroom.

Once I'm in the men's room I hear that stupid teen soap theme song again as my zComm starts to vibrate in a manner more painful than usual. Pretty soon I'm hit with a wave of digital information that lets me know that Svetlana is secretly working as an undercover agent for Tetrace and that she means to steal the Spartak Trigger for them as soon as Kirill retrieves it from his safety deposit box in Budapest. I ask for some college basketball scores and whatever flunky's manning the controls at MetroTech shoots them into my brain for me.

THE SPARTAK TRIGGER

I storm into the women's room and catch Svetlana whispering something into a tiny hand-held receiver. She tucks the device into her jacket as soon as she sees me and an outlandishly-incredulous expression somehow augments her beauty. *Wow.*

"What do you want?" she near-yelps.

"Who were you talking to right there?"

"I don't know what you're talking about. I was just checking my makeup."

"So you weren't just explaining to the dicks following us on Tetra-Earth why we've stopped here in Godollo?"

She peers at me disdainfully and asks me who I'm working for. "The CIA?" I shake my head. "MI-6?" I shake my head. "The Mossad?"

"Do I look like a fucking Heeb to you, bitch?"

"You do a little bit actually."

"I do?"

"Yes."

"No one's ever told me that before."

"It's not the kind of thing that would come up in conversation often."

"I suppose not."

"So what do we do now?"

I take my pistol out and tell her not to move. "Don't even blink, honey." I back up to the washroom room door and open it with my free hand prior to propping it open with my foot, keeping my gun fixed on Svetlana the whole time. Kirill's finished gassing up and paying and I shout for him to drive up to the station's lavatory area, which he does. Soon the whole of Black October has joined us in the women's room. When they find me with a pistol pointed at Svetlana they all take their guns out and point them at me, even Conrad.

"What are you doing in the lady's bathroom, Peter?" Mikhail asks me, gruffly.

"Excellent question, my dimwitted friend. I was going to try and force this slut in here to give me a hand job but instead I caught her giving capitalist imperialism a nice sloppy BJ!"

Kirill gives me an intense, angry look and asks me what the hell I'm talking about as he pulls the hammer back on his revolver and takes a menacing step towards me. I quickly tell him the woman he loves has been feeding information to a powerful American company that wants to get their greasy hands on the Spartak Trigger and that she's going to betray us all once we get to Budapest, steal the microfilm, and deliver to them.

"How do you know this?" Vasiliy asks me.

"I caught her speaking into a transmitter. It's in her jacket right now, go ahead and check."

"He's lying!" Svetlana shrieks, shrewdly pulling out the device and holding it up over her head. "He is the one who is planning on betraying us to Tetrace. He planted this transmitter on me at gunpoint in order to frame me and draw attention away from himself!" She turns to face her fiancé and adopts a piteous, desperate tone. "Think Kirill, how in the name of god do you think he knew about us in the first place?! They sent him here to infiltrate our group and steal your destiny from you!"

The narrator seems confused as to whether we're undergoing peripeteia or anagnorisis or neither at the moment but I don't have time to help him figure it out since Svetlana just served up a big juicy "I Never Said It Was Poison" trope. Well, kinda. Close enough for our purposes anyway...

"Nice try, sugartits!" I shout, trying to sound like a prosecutor catching a witness in a lie on the stand. "I didn't say it was Tetrace who's after the microfilm. I just said it was a big American company."

Kirill lowers his gun and looks over at Svetlana in disgust. He tells Mikhail and Vasiliy to take her out of his sight. They quickly advance upon her and she starts to scream for help so Mikhail puts his big meat hook of a paw over her mouth and drags her flailing body out of the concrete room.

"Don't worry," I say, putting my hand on Kirill's shoulder amicably. "There's plenty of fish in the sea, kid."

"Fuck you, Peter."

THE SPARTAK TRIGGER

I'm about to apologize to Kirill for trying to score a wrister from his fiancée before we discovered that she was a traitorous mole when Mikhail cries out in pain from the outside. We rush out to see what's happened and find him kneeling on the ground with his face covered in blood. "The bitch bit my ear off!" he yelps, holding the detached appendage up for us to see.

Vasiliy is rolling around on the ground next to him, clutching his groin. "And she kicked me in the balls," he moans.

We all look up in unison and see Svetlana escaping into an assuredly-horny truck driver's massive rig.

"Does she know which bank you've got the mircrofilm stashed at?" Conrad asks Kirill.

"No," he replies flatly. "She doesn't."

Conrad: "Well then, we'd better move quickly before she gets in touch with her pals at Tetrace and figures it out."

"We need to switch vehicles too," I chime in. "They're liable to be tracking us with Tetra-Earth right now."

"Goddamn Super Apps!!" Kirill snaps, kicking our vehicle's front bumper as hard as he can. The Alexeis help Mikhail and Vasiliy get into the van while Conrad rushes into the convenience store to purchase an ear-sized bandage from the deviant cashier.

《《《—》》》

Kirill's a tightly-wound ball of nerves by the time we get to Budapest in our hot cargo van. The city's a lot bigger and nicer than I figured it would be. We zoom past a bunch of pretty sweet pre-modern architecture on our way to the bank where the microfilm's stashed. I make mental notes of spots I'd like to visit someday if I ever come back here, which I know full-well will never happen. Probably not anyway.

We pull into a parking garage pretty close to the Danube River and Kirill tells us he'll be back in a few minutes. I think about getting out right now and stealing the Spartak Trigger from him as soon as he retrieves it from the bank vault but quickly decide not to. Even with my new super karate skills and shit it'd be a tall order to take out all five of these fuckers and god knows Conrad wouldn't be much help. *Patience man, patience.* "Fuck you," I mutter to myself.

"Who are you talking to?" Mikhail asks me.

"You, now."

"Do not push me, Western scum. You caught Vasiliy and I by surprise back at the bar in Omsk. The next time we fight you won't be so fortunate."

"Take it easy Slick—we're on the same team, remember?"

"I'll make a note of it."

Conrad starts whispering something important-sounding to me but I ignore him and announce that I'm getting some fresh air. I force open the rear door and hop out of our freezing-cold van just as Kirill shows up and slides back into the driver's seat.

"Where are you going, Peter?" he asks me.

"I was going to pick up a Hungarian cigar. I've heard good things about them."

"What the hell are you talking about? Get back in the van!"

"Mind your tone, comrade. Don't forget who financed this little road trip of ours."

I can tell Kirill doesn't like being addressed in such a firm manner under such tense circumstances and he fires a big league scowl at me, like that's supposed to intimidate me or something. "Did you get the microfilm?" I ask him as I jump back into my seat between the Alexeis.

He reaches into his jacket pocket and pulls out a small black cylinder. The back of my head starts to tingle and the narrator starts speaking in a muffled, passionate tone, as if he's recording the voiceover for a melodramatic film trailer. Team Black October starts celebrating as Kirill jams a screw driver back into the van's ignition key and fires the engine back up.

"And the wire transfer went through?" Alexei #2 asks. "Did you get the coordinates of Hilmar's laboratory?"

"Yes, of course, now let's get out of this goddamned city and figure out how the fuck we're going to make it to Austria."

"Good plan, boss," Mikhail snivels. Brown-noser.

《《《—》》》

I ask a bunch of questions about the computer lab we're going to as we get back on the highway and make our way out of Budapest. Kirill patronizes me to a point but then he gets pissed off and demands to be left alone with his thoughts.

Vasiliy tells me I need to be respectful of our leader and I tell him to fuck off and he takes his gun out and so do I. "Goddamn it, you're like a bunch of children!" Kirill exclaims, angrily slamming his palms upon the steering wheel. "Can you please just get along with each other long enough for us to get to Salzburg?! For Christ's sake, come on!!"

We apologize in sheepish unison and Kirill thanks us for obliging his wishes. He then releases a heavy sigh whose diffusion gives birth to a disgruntled silence that lives just long enough to witness a transport truck smash into us from the side and run us off the road into a ditch.

《《《—》》》

Our van's lying upside down on the ground and a smoldering grey vapor is making its way through the cabin. My head is throbbing and my vision's blurred but I can definitely hear footsteps and voices approaching.

"Anyone alive in here?" I ask, almost shouting. A few groggily-delivered responses let me know I'm not the only survivor. The muffled footsteps continue to approach, threateningly. I hear a distant voice issue a command to be careful not to damage the microfilm and to only shoot at our heads since Kirill could've given the cylinder to any one of us. After a second or two I realize that it's Svetlana speaking and I manage to wrangle myself out of my seatbelt and fall onto the floor/ceiling. I free Conrad from his seat and he's not conscious so I check his pulse to see if he's alive. Yup. I open the side door and drag Conrad out onto the snow-covered ground before drawing my gun and firing blindly into the smoke-riddled scene before me. There's a smattering of retaliatory gunfire and I duck down and cut my hands on some broken glass as I crawl back into the van.

"Help me, Peter," Mikhail begs from the back seat. I grab him by the shoulders and pull him out of the wreckage. Both of the Alexeis are unconscious and Vasiliy has a large shard of glass sticking out of his neck. He's completely covered in blood. I tell Mikhail to fire his gun into the air and he does so, prompting another round of gunfire from the Tetrites which is quickly silenced as Svetlana again barks at them to be careful about hitting the microfilm. *Why the hell did she have them run us off the road then?? Stupid bitch.*

I make my way into the front seat and Kirill's eyes are wide open but he doesn't seem to be breathing. I reach up into his jacket to grab the microfilm and I'm shocked when his hand springs to life and grabs mine. "What…happened…Peter?" Kirill manages to ask me between prolonged gasps. I tell him that Svetlana and her friends from Tetrace ran us off the road and now they're advancing on us trying to get their hands on the Spartak Trigger.

"Don't…let them…have it," he pleads, mumbling something about his precious revolutionary cause with his final breath. I pry the canister from Kirill's dead hand and tell him I'll see him in Russian Hell as I squirm back out of the overturned vehicle.

Conrad's awake now but Mikhail's passed out. Svetlana shouts out and tells us that if we give them the microfilm they'll let us live. I look at Conrad and his eyes are completely blank for the first time since I've met him. He begins to cry and I tell him to stop being such a pussy before announcing to Svetlana that we're willing to accept their terms. "Just give us a minute to gather our things and tend to our wounded!"

THE SPARTAK TRIGGER

"You have exactly one minute then…comrade!"

"So we're just going to give them the microfilm?" Conrad asks me, desperately.

"I guess so, yeah. You have a better idea on how we get out of this?"

The narrator mentions that weird Latin phrase again and all of a sudden there's a fucking helicopter flying towards us. I can hear the Tetrace crew clamoring excitedly and then a super loud machine gun starts going off and tears the lot of them to pieces, Svetlana included. The chopper makes its way over to where we're crouched down and one of those rope ladders gets thrown overboard and it hits Mikhail right in the groin. Luckily for him, he's dead now and doesn't feel a thing.

Conrad grabs the handles first and starts to slowly climb the ladder. "Get the lead out, dude!" I yell beneath the black rotorcraft's deafening propeller. We eventually both climb into the chopper's main cabin and a battle fatigue-clad Tristan Miller and Dickie Gunn are there to greet us. "Good to go, Reggie!" Miller shouts and we start flying forward as the narrator laments the fact that he's run out of plot coupons and I guess he goes off to retrieve some more.

«««—»»»

Dickie asks me for the Spartak Trigger and I ask him about the two million dollars MetroTech promised me. "You'll get it, don't worry!" he yells. I hand him the microfilm and both he and Miller cry out with delight. "That's the stuff dreams are made of boys," I say, doing my best Humphrey Bogart impression.

"You've made our bosses very happy Mister Bishop," Dickie tells me.

"That's great," I reply. For some reason you skip ahead to the epilogue and discover that the dead Russian spy was actually a double-agent working for the CIA and the "algorithm" on his microfilm was just a recipe for meatloaf. You also learn that

MetroTech goes out of business in a few years after the whole zComm thing proves to be a disaster. Looks like Tetrace also ends up going bankrupt after they get busted trying orchestrate another massive identity theft scam involving a digital crime protection company called LifeSafe that idiots subscribe to for some reason. Whatever.

"Wait, your name's Bishop?" Conrad asks me, perplexed.

"Used to be, yeah."

"Who's your friend?" Miller asks. "He looks familiar."

"He should, dumbass. This is Horace Conrad, digital terrorist extraordinaire."

"So it is." Miller smiles awkwardly. "How the hell did you two hook up?"

"Your boy Pavel introduced us back in Russia," I say, suddenly craving a stiff drink. "He sends his regards by the way."

The pilot hits an air pocket and the resulting turbulence causes Conrad to throw up into a football helmet that's on board for some reason.

«««—»»»

Dickie and Miller drop me off at an airport in some town called Zalakros and tell me I'm booked on a midnight flight to Heathrow where I'll be able to hop on a connection back to the states. "I'm still wanted for murder at home you know," I tell them.

"Yeah, we know," Miller says. "I guess you can stay here in Europe if you want. Pretty sure that Russian identity we set you up with is still good."

"I guess I'll do that then. What about him?" I point to Conrad, who looks utterly dejected.

"There's a five million Euro reward for turning this guy in," Dickie tells me, patting Conrad on the back. "So we're going to do that, get this microfilm back to the brass at MetroTech, then Tristan and I are gonna retire someplace tropical."

THE SPARTAK TRIGGER

"What are you guys—gay together or something?" I ask.

"Yeah," they say harmoniously.

"Gross. Well look, can you homos make that sure MetroTech wires half the money they owe me to Iris Elizabeth Bishop in Surprise, Arizona?"

"Sure thing Bishop," Dickie says. "What about the other million?"

I pull out the credit card Miller gave me and tell them to put the rest of the balance on there for me to use. "Can you program any more useful shit into me before you leave?" I ask Miller.

"Nope," he says. "Your zComm unit's been damaged actually. That car crash must've dislodged the interface hookup. You're totally offline."

"Even better. Well, good luck being gay on your private island, guys."

"Thanks," Miller and Dickie say, again in unison.

"Oh yeah," Dickie says. "I almost forgot." He produces a standard-sized envelope and hands it to me. "This came for you at MetroTech headquarters, looks like it's your Super Budget Discount Rewards Club membership card."

"Awesome," I snatch the envelope from his hand and shove it in my pocket. "Thanks."

I say goodbye to Conrad and wish him luck in prison. I ask him what he's going to do while he's in there and he says he's going to write a book based upon our adventures together in Europe.

"Nice," I say. "What's the title gonna be?"

He thinks about it for a moment before responding with a level of zeal that surprises everyone: *The Aristocrats!*"

Bryce Allen was born in Atlantic Canada in the early-1980s. He graduated from the University of King's College in 2004 with a BA in History and currently resides in the Midwestern United States. *The Spartak Trigger* is his first published novel.

TheSpartakTrigger.com

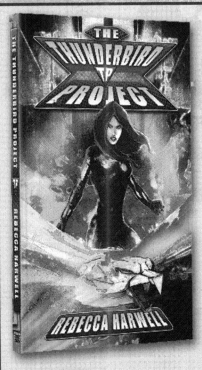

NOT ALL SUPERHEROES LIVE A GLAMOROUS LIFE.

The Thunderbird project was an FBI-run group of superhumans until they were unceremoniously disbanded and sent out into the world to live normal lives. But unfortunately for the red-headed, mean-tempered Jupiter being 18-foot tall makes blending into society pretty much impossible. She resigns herself to living in warehouses and searching for a place where she can just be left alone.

SOME JUST WANT THE WORLD TO FORGET THEM.

Four years later, after being followed for days by unmarked vehicles, Jupiter is attacked and left for dead on a bridge, narrowly rescued amidst screams and camera flashes by an old teammate. She discovers that members of The Thunderbird Project are being targeted and one is already dead. Jupiter reluctantly joins the newly reinstated group.

BUT SOME PEOPLE WON'T FORGET AND JUST WANT THEM DEAD.

With a whole lot of pain and past between them, the team struggles to find the identity of the assassins so they can all go back home. Since any chance of getting away from the world disappeared the day she crawled onto that bridge, Jupiter just wants to make the guys who came after her pay. And if that means sticking it to a world that hates her...so much the better.

YOU DON'T GET A 'HAPPILY EVER AFTER' WHEN EVERYONE CONSIDERS YOU A FREAK.

eBook • Trade Paperback • Hardcover

BEDLAM PRESS
WWW.BEDLAMPRESS.COM

Cristina Nichols fears the future, through the harrowing whispers of her past. She longs to forget the depraved abuses she suffered in her youth that left her afraid of love and passion. But something, somewhere, is suddenly tantalizing her, beckoning into a muse of carnal revelation and ecstatic fulfillment...

SECRET PASSIONS...

Deep in the cryptic New York City brownstone, something awakens, brimming with hot, real breath, libidinous longings and desires of the flesh the likes of which Cristina cannot conceive...

A SECRET LUST BURIED FOR AGES...

In the basement she finds it, the sinister evil finally unbound, reaching forth in vampiric bloodlust to prey upon her most forbidden fantasies and plummet her body and soul into a chasm of wantonness as black as the most timeless sin...

IMPALER

The secret will drench your desires in blood...

AVAILABLE IN TRADE PAPERBACK AND EBOOK

WWW.NECROPUBLICATIONS.COM

> Ye serpents,
> Ye generation of vipers,
> How can ye escape
> The damnation of
> Gehenna?
> - Matthew 23:33

1879

The outlaw Jedediah Sykes has just killed the wrong man, the nephew of a powerful rail baron. Now he's on the run and the bounty hunter Jacob Hatcher is hot on his trail with a group of hired men and Apache guides. But when the guides refuse to go any further, warning that the lands ahead are cursed by an ancient and nameless evil, Jacob is forced to go the trail alone–a trail that leads him to a town, a dark paradise of sin and vice called Gehenna.

Hatcher and Sykes soon become entangled in the mysteries of Gehenna's peculiar denizens: a fire & brimstone Jesuit who's preaching to a city of lost souls, and a shadowy figure who rules over the town like a living god. When one of them makes a choice that threatens to damn them all, the rest must work together to find a stolen key that can unlock the domain of the dead. And in their search, confront not only their own demons, but the hidden horrors of Gehenna itself.

EBOOK • TRADE PAPERBACK • HARDCOVER
WEIRD WEST BOOKS
WWW.WEIRDWESTBOOKS.COM

"All folklore is based on some remnants of truth, the Bible is no exception... The Horsemen are very real, they are immortal, and their only goal is to feed on mankind's suffering and enslave humanity."

An elementary school full of kids destroyed by a tornado... A soldier makes it home from the Middle East only to be killed for his wallet... A mother of three diagnosed with metastatic breast cancer... Random events? NO.

Photojournalist Faye Monroe discovers that the ugliness and cruelty afflicting the world does not arise of its own actions: the countless wars, the outbreaks of disease and natural disasters, even the murder of her friends and family—the work of malevolent architects.

THEY ARE UNLEASHED!

War, Death, Disease and Famine... The Four Horsemen have fed the world endless despair for millennia. But one of them has been destroyed and its spirit seeks a new host.

Faye, together with a Mossad agent and a rebel assassin, quickly plunge into danger, intrigue and supernatural adventure as the trio search for the key to save Faye's soul...and hopefully prevent Armageddon.

A riveting and breakneck supernatural thriller.

EBOOK • TRADE PAPERBACK • HARDCOVER

BEDLAM PRESS
WWW.BEDLAMPRESS.COM

THERE ARE THINGS EVEN ANGELS AND DAEMONS FEAR...

"I would have absolutely no hesitation in recommending this book to anyone who has even the most tenuous affection for Fantasy. For those of us that love fantasy with a true and unrelenting passion, then this will not disappoint. In fact it may even reaffirm those who may have become jaded and somewhat disillusioned with fantasy and horror in this post-Twilight sparkly world that we inhabit."

— UK Horror Scene

There's a war going on...

...a war for human souls, and the only weapons allowed are whispers and nudges.

Do you believe in angels and daemons? It doesn't really matter, because they believe in you.

From innocuous suburban homes where madness festers like rotten meat, to the Gardens of Avalon where the grass is green and the sun always shines; from the corrupt back-alleys of London, to any small American town...they are there.

And they're fighting over you...

Nathalie is an angel: beautiful, powerful beyond belief and in charge of stopping people from doing anything too evil...as long as she plays by the rules, that is. Free will is considered of upmost importance by the powers that be, and Intervention is frowned upon severely with a plunge to the fires below as punishment.

And the daemons? Well, they're in charge of the tempting, of course.

When Jason, a fallen angel with flawless looks and an even more flawless tailored suit, sets his sights on tempting someone with more to lose than any human, will Nathalie have the strength of will to resist Intervention? And if she does fall, what will become of her?

There are things even angels and daemons fear...

Nathalie's journey through sin, temptation, and free will explores how far you are prepared to go to stop good people doing bad things. If you stop someone pulling the trigger, does that mean that in their heart they didn't commit murder?

Sometimes...the best things are done by the worst people.

EBOOK • TRADE PAPERBACK • HARDCOVER
BEDLAM PRESS
WWW.BEDLAMPRESS.COM

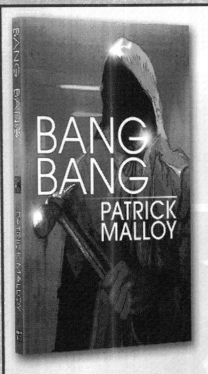

Youthimax is a cure-all miracle drug from Johnson and Johnson which has all but eliminated death in modern society. Which is great news. Unless you work at a funeral home.

So Darkly Funny You'll Want To Hit Someone In the Face... With A Hammer!

The O'Rourke Funeral Home in West Philadelphia has fallen into obscurity, along with it's two sole employees. Max and Bligh waste the days away sleeping in coffins and counting shovels until that fateful day that they decide to become serial killers. The drunken Bligh finds serendipitous instructions in the Beatles tune "Maxwell's Silver Hammer" and convinces his partner that it's only right that Maxwell kill with a silver hammer. With little business and less regret, Maxwell and his alcoholic train wreck of a partner become the most infamous serial killers in Philadelphia history. Business is booming in both the funeral home and the serial killing industries as the world searches for these Beatles killers.

In a perfect world, serial killers could do their jobs unencumbered. But the world isn't perfect, and the duo are soon weighed down with a nosey Mafioso, an uncontrollable teen daughter, the funeral home's bitter elderly owner, and the F.B.I. Obviously, comedy abounds.

Bang Bang has everything a dark comedy should have including, but not limited to: murder, love, murder, alcohol, murder, stereotyping, murder, Beatles music, murder, family, murder, public transportation, and even murder. In case you haven't figured it out, there's a whole lotta murder in this book.

Will the F.B.I. catch the killers?
Will the mafia get to the murderers first?
Will Paul McCartney sue this writer?
Find out in *Bang Bang*, the hilariously untrue story of funeral home serial killers and hammer hijinks. And Vaseline! All of your non-Paul-McCartney-lawsuit questions are answered in this brilliant debut novel, written in the style of a poorly educated Mark Twain!

EBOOK • TRADE PAPERBACK • HARDCOVER
BEDLAM PRESS
WWW.BEDLAMPRESS.COM

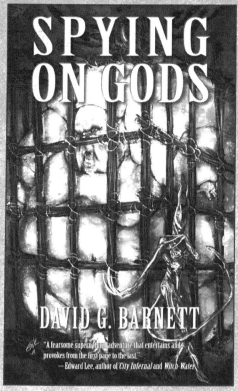

A drunken, naked frenzy leads to a nightmare summoned to earth. A nightmare not meant to be witnessed by human eyes. Because if it is, the village will pay–and pay it does.

When the villagers find a broken man on the forest floor they know he's to blame for the curse that's befallen them, and they want his blood. Now, helped along by some sympathetic villagers, he's on a frantic race for his life and sanity. But the road to redemption leads them straight into the mouth of a hellish realm and the arms of an ancient god–benevolent until its rules are broken. And the group will soon find out the cost for...

SPYING ON GODS

"This is dark/occult fantasy with powerful new twists, viewpoint, and tangents whose sub-text throws Thomas Aquinas, J.P. Sartre, and John Milton into a blender and unloads the wicked concoction onto an unsuspecting reader's head. Part grotesque morality play, part ethereal allegory, part alternate-mythology, all glued excitingly together with earthy ancient diabolism and exquisitely morbid horror. A fearsome supernatural adventure that entertains and provokes from the first page to the last."
– Edward Lee, author of *City Infernal* and *The Bighead*

WWW.NECROPUBLICATIONS.COM

Made in the USA
Lexington, KY
05 November 2014